THE
INDIGO
TRAIL

THE INDIGO TRAIL

The Crystals of Change

AMANDA RYAN

FIRST EDITION

ISBNs

978-1-80227-764-7 (eBook)

978-1-80227-765-4 (paperback)

To my children Josh, Gabriella, Georgie and Saskia

For the gift of pride and opening my mind to new worlds, for showing me that it does not matter that a square peg can never be hammered into a round hole because there is magic in that.

To my husband Greg, for taking the hammer out of my hand and replacing it with endless cups of tea, for his steadfast love and support and for putting up with crazy.

To Mum and Dad, Eileen and Barry, for living long lives as a constant and strength, giving me my work ethic formed during my early character building years, also for the yummiest gravy and for putting magic into Christmas. Mum, you were the 'Hostess with the Mostess' for so many glorious fun-filled family gatherings. These memories will always shine brightly and my heart is full when I think of them. Dad, you imbued me with a sense of mischief, an inner steel, a perpetual power pack of determination and to fly my kite so high (2,100 feet of kite string!) that we needed binoculars to see it!

To Nick and Duncan for piggy backs, 'big brother protection' and for spending all your school trip money buying me a 'Chi Chi' panda when I was too young to go.

To Terry for teaching that Pooh Bear wisdom is the greatest of all and for making me laugh when I felt like crying.

Also, to Bowie, our black Labrador, for not minding when I pretend to be his voice, his hugs on demand and for thinking I am a better person than I could ever hope to be.

CONTENTS

Acknowledgements

'The first word is the hardest,' said Greg, my husband, 'there is never a right time to write.'

I remember it well. It was a dreary winter's day and my mood matched, frustrated by my loss of self, and lack of value. I was one of a dying breed of professionals turned full time mother of four and 'housewife.' When children are young and demanding, there is always a so-called better time and an excuse to delay, so I thank Greg for that pick-me-up conversation that spawned the germ of an idea for this story and made me write that very first word. 'Write' being the operative word since my story would come alive largely during time spent waiting in the car for my children, using a notebook I had designated for the job, but also on random bits of paper such as used envelopes and till receipts.

At the heart of this life chapter is how all-consuming it can be to navigate a previously unexplored world as a new parent when only the unpredictable becomes predictable, and something may seem impossible until the first time you have done it. That is what happens when you have little people counting on you. This story takes its influence from watching my children

Josh, Gabriella, Georgie and Saskia grow up to one day collect their wings and fly free. I am indebted to them for enriching my life in ways I had never considered, and in their unwitting contribution to giving my writing its heartbeat. They are the difference to anything I ever imagined parenting to be, introducing me to another way of thinking and teaching me more about life than all my years of formal education. They taught me that success takes many forms. I was educated and yet ignorant. I thought life was easy: stick to the rules, work hard, act smart what could be simpler? To those around me who may have been struggling, possibly disillusioned by being bottom of the class, or crushed at being the last left standing to be chosen for a team, although aware of their disappointment and humiliation, in retrospect I remained so unashamedly uninformed. My thinking was so superficial, that these people should just try a bit harder. It took having children and encountering the autistic spectrum for the first time that I became aware of so many other layers to most situations. I was compelled to open my eyes and to broaden my mind and begin to understand what makes us all so different and that it is something to acknowledge and celebrate. I will be honest that it came as a shock, taking me clean out of my comfort zone to navigate unchartered waters, finding our way through the complex maze of the autistic spectrum with its many nuances and idiosyncrasies.

I would like to express deep love and utmost admiration to my first born and gentle soul, Josh. His brilliant mind, sharp wit and the invaluable insights he gave me into feeling the outsider, fuelled this important theme in The Indigo Trail. Throughout most of his primary school years, Josh had a severe speech impediment. For the first time I was committed to something truly worthy when after years of regular speech therapy sessions and home exercises, his therapist was thinking we should call it a day, that until Josh had maturation of his jaw as a young adult, any progress would be negligible. I felt helpless. The bullies were merciless in their mimicry and ridicule of Josh who with his polite, gentle manner presented as such an easy target, and with High School on the horizon, we both dreaded what may lie in store. Nevertheless, it was as if the sleeping lion had been prodded with a great big stick and stirred to action; I devised my own original strategies and exercises to help Josh articulate the sounds he had always found difficult, despite his youngest sibling, Saskia, toddling past and cheekily saying them for him as if it was one big game! We worked tirelessly every day for several hours, sometimes laughing, sometimes crying and often frustrated, but it was a few months down the road, that his speech therapist, confounded by my son's clear speech, declared 10-year-old Josh to be a 'mini miracle' and signed him off. Less than a year later, Josh landed a leading role in an all-child cast feature film from over 8000 auditionees. His speech was never in question. I would further like to thank Josh for his structural edit of my early manuscript that I took on board and implemented. He has an astute literary mind and is always there in the background as a loyal and loving Labrador of a human being and a wonderful son.

I also extend my extreme gratitude to my trio of girls for the invaluable lessons they have taught me and for being understanding that I was not good with hair and girly stuff, and so learned in a flash to French plait, high ponytail or bun their hair to spare us all the embarrassment! I thank Gabriella for her angelic glow of constant kindness that conceals a steely determination. Anyone who saw Gabriella, at 8 years of age, in a gymnastics competition perilously clinging beneath a balance beam claw her way back onto the top of the apparatus without touching down to avoid a penalty 'fall' deduction, will understand why I find her inner strength so inspiring. Everyone applauded rapturously that day at the awesome grit of a tiny human and whenever a further edit felt like another unwanted uphill battle that I questioned, this image of Gabriella came into my head, inspiring me to dig deep and to get the job done. She is my light on the darkest of days, including those with writers block.

Georgie, or the 'G Bomb' as I like to call her, showed me that sometimes the rules are to be broken, the magic that can come from outside the box thinking, and that being unconventional often leads to exciting roads. I channelled her spirit into my protagonist, Tiggy, the indigo child. Try to manipulate an indigo child and show authority and the chances are you will not succeed. Three-year-old Georgie taught me this when my early attempts to persuade and cajole backfired and resulted in her using her wile to skilfully hide, not just one, but both sets of car keys. I hunted all day panicked by the impending afternoon school pick-up for her older siblings whilst she watched, quivering like a jelly on a plate with laughter at my hopeless attempts to find them. They eventually turned up in a seldom-used bookcase of adult books, carefully placed behind the wooden doorframe so that mere glancing into the glass doors would draw a blank. I learnt a very big lesson that day. Georgie, like the protagonist, Tiggy, makes the world come in line and will be the change in you. She is my wonderful unicorn in a field of horses.

My gratitude would be far from complete without mentioning my youngest daughter who as a little one insisted she was called 'Saskia Star.' I was her 'Big Panda' and she was my 'Little Panda' and my sunshine on a rainy day because she was always smiling. To Saskia I owe much gratitude (and a lifetime of marmite on toast!) for her sunny patience sat beside me in our leaky Fiat Multipla, waiting for her siblings to appear from dance and drama classes or a guitar lesson. I thank her for all the 'Tic Tac' races (a challenge to make a single Tic Tac mint last the longest) during this time, even though she always won. Her self-sufficiency and easy-going nature gave me the time to write. Mature beyond her years Saskia was from earliest days, my dependable, fair-minded, sensible little friend.

Four special and unique individuals, all very different but each has played an important part in opening my mind to new ways of thinking and challenging what I had always thought and assumed to be right when sometimes I was wrong. Now their wisdom is our wisdom just as the adults in The Indigo Trail similarly have lessons to learn.

Finally, words of appreciation for Greg, my husband who from our first meeting over forty years ago, has always been my best friend and my rock. He is quite simply, my man for all seasons and all reasons and has made me feel like a 10 feet tall sunflower when in reality I am more of a daisy!

I thank all of the above for their endless love and support, for enriching my life in ways I had never thought possible and making me feel a more complete and, hopefully, better person along the way. It has been these very special people who have inspired my storytelling and have supported me to the end. The Indigo Trail would be nothing without them.

Chapter 1

THE STORM

There is a last time for everything for everyone.

There is always that last summer, a last catch up with a friend, a last glance in the mirror and that last kiss. The good thing though is that there is a last time for the grim stuff, too, like sitting in the dentist's chair for a filling or walking into the exam room. Whether you are a real Queen, or just a drama queen, the fastest or slowest, strongest or weakest, there is no filter. Famous person, scientific genius or charity champion, it doesn't matter. 'The last time' is a common thread to us all. We cannot escape it.

Nevertheless, there is a 'but', and this is a very big 'but', if you knew when that 'last time' was, would you do anything differently? Scroll back a hundred years and put yourself in the shoes of somebody ordinary, on an ordinary day in an extraordinary time. World War I had made everyone mindful of 'the last time', especially that 'last goodbye.' Is it really any surprise that after the chaos and tragedy of 'The Great War' (like there was anything 'great' about it!) that people wanted to live a bit, conscious of 'the last time'?

It was 'The Roaring Twenties', the Flapper Age of 'The New Woman,' who smoked, drank (and thanks to a group of lioness-hearted females), now even voted. They tried to celebrate life rather than simply remembering death, choosing to live each day as if it were their last, the last time for everything. It had been bleak. What a nonsense it is to talk about 'winning the war' and 'who won the war?' We have all heard it said, but seriously, who wins?

The 1920s may seem a long time ago but certain things remain the same: boys fancied girls, girls fancied boys and every other combination (that was either lied about or denied) and the desire to love and be loved still mattered as much then as they do now. Think about it! Everyone is the star in one's own life story. Time itself may create a different backdrop to the action but the character at heart remains the same. It just does.

That is why a decade on from the last gunshots ringing out, in a humble kitchen in a humble village, a family was just getting on and doing, living each day mindful of that last time, that last goodbye. It was '10th birthday eve' for twins, Arnold and Arthur Ramsbottom. An iced birthday cake stood on the kitchen dresser alongside the rather fabulous Marconi radio. Apart from Shadow, the family's black Labrador, the radio was by far their most treasured possession. Owning such a coveted item had real bragging rights, not that anything much was audible above the horrendous crackle. 'A Cold Dark Night' was playing. If it had been clearer the boys might have heard the haunting twanging of a slide guitar and Blind Willie Johnson's pained humming. It could have been an omen that something bad, very bad, was about to happen, a warning for the twins to stay indoors. It was indeed, a cold, dark night.

'Hope we get candles!' said Arthur putting on his coat and fastening the buttons.

'We will! Ma hid them in the pantry,' responded Arnold, the oldest twin by ten minutes. 'I heard her singing that new 'Happy Birthday' song that Auntie Mabel told her about.'

Arnold was about to break off a tiny piece of the cake's icing.

'Don't, Ma will kill you!' warned Arthur smacking his brother's hand.

'Hope she doesn't cut a piece for Hugh again,' said Arnold, his eyes moving to a knife and fork set beside a clean plate on a table of dirty dishes left over from their evening meal.

Shadow nuzzled against the boys' legs. He seemed to have an in-built clock when it was time for his walk. Arnold nodded.

'I reckon she will. Ma just won't accept that Hugh is never coming back,' Arthur said.

'I know,' agreed Arnold sneaking a tiny spike of icing into his mouth. 'How different things would be if we still had our big brother. Wish Hugh was here!'

'It 'ud mend Mum's heart,' Arthur said putting on a black hand knitted balaclava and passing his brother the same in grey. 'Wish we'd known him.'

'Stupid war!' the twins said simultaneously.

Shadow whimpered, starting to get impatient.

'All right, all right!' said Arthur taking hold of his lead and turning off the radio before closing the door behind them.

It was a wild, cold night, both windy and rainy. The boys trudged across the farmland in their clodhopper boots doing what they could to keep warm, but even their brotherly love felt cold in this. They shared secrets and pretended to smoke with sticks. One twin was dark and the other was fair. Otherwise, they looked alike although Arthur always dressed in black and Arnold in grey for all those extra bits like hats, gloves and socks. In the distance, the village church clock was striking six but the boys took no notice of it. They heard the clock every single day. Maybe if they had known that for one boy he would be hearing them for the very last time they would have stopped to listen.

'Cor! Look at this!' exclaimed Arnold, picking up a dead firework off the muddy ground. He sniffed the gunpowder shell breathing it in like an intoxicating scent.

'Smell it!' he said passing it to his brother.

Arthur inhaled deeply.

'Let's keep it!' he said putting the burnt-out Roman candle shell into his pocket.

The twins ploughed on over the farmland that had turned into a hunting ground as the boys looked for more shells to collect as if they were treasure.

'That storm is coming! It's been building up all day,' Arthur said but continuing to walk further away from home. 'That was thunder!'

'Go back?' asked Arnold.

The wind was like a savage monster on the prowl for a kill. There was no care for age, family or anything but wanting to destroy. The boys took courage from each other. It was a twin thing and having one another made the brothers that little bit braver. In fact, they had quite a reputation for daring to do things that other kids thought crazy and were known as 'The Baloney Boys' because they talked baloney and made stuff up.

'Let's tell people the wind blew us into a ditch!' said Arnold.

'Or that the lightning got us?' Arthur suggested seeming excited by the idea.

Shadow ran up and sniffed his pocket, snorting at the gunpowder scent. The dog seemed unsettled. The storm raged on but despite this, the twins were having a good time. They chatted about their 'love lists,' the girls they fancied that week and their birthday the next day, jumping about excitedly like a bag of frogs.

'Hope we get a balloon!' said Arthur trying to catch his breath that was vaporising into clouds in the cold air.

'Fat chance!' replied Arnold also trying to catch his own misty breaths. 'Who d'ya know that's had one of those?'

So much of life is about timing and the choices we make. For instance, whether we manage to catch the bus or miss the bus and the events that may then unravel. Some say it is fate, written in the stars and that everything happens for a reason. Who knows! Sometimes the smallest decisions are big life changers as the twins were about to discover. The storm had intensified and was behaving like a bully. The thunder crashed and lightning flashed, lighting up the feeble earth beneath it. This was Nature bossing the Earth and winning.

'Gawd blimey, that wind sounds like wolves,' said Arnold.

'Hungry wolves,' Arthur added tugging on his brother's coat to get him to take shelter with him beneath a large oak tree.

He took out a penknife from his pocket and began to carve letters into the tree trunk trying to distract himself from the storm. The boys put on a brave face but inside their stomachs churned as the thunder boomed above them. They didn't speak. There was no need. The twins knew they were feeling the same.

Summer had been a scorcher with barely any rain but now, sun kissed, golden days seemed as out of reach to the boys as trying to remember somebody that they had never met before.

'The sheep don't like it!' muttered Arnold, listening to their distant cries coming from the Derbyshire's farm.

'It's like a storm in a horror movie, like Frankenstein,' said Arthur pulling a gruesome face.

'Or Dr. Jekyll and Mr. Hyde,' added Arnold watching his brother carving a 'true love' heart for the girl at the top of his 'love list.'

The church clock struck again. This time seven long tolls rang out. They were so haunting in the storm and sounded so different to hearing them in nicer weather.

'Quasimodo!' Arthur teased hunching his back beneath his coat. 'I live in the church bell tower,' he said pointing into the darkness towards the shadowy outline of the church and then nervously giggling.

The truth was that both boys were scared and in trying to take their minds off the situation, they were making themselves feel even worse. Another symphony of beating rain and claps of thunder blasted out. The twins grabbed each other.

'It's raining, it's pouring, the old man is snoring,' sang Arnold fiddling with his balaclava because the wool irritated his skin. 'He went to bed and he bumped his head and couldn't get up in the morning.' I reckon we should leg it. Ma will be getting worried.'

'Ma's not here drowning!' grumbled Arthur.

'Last one back is a sissy!' challenged Arnold making a move. Arthur stood firm and yanked his brother back by his arm.

'All right let's toss for it!' said Arthur fumbling in his pockets and taking out a coin.

'Bagsy call!' replied Arnold feeling a bit cheesed off.

Usually, an answer or decision from one of them was as good as an answer or decision from the other. However, in the storm this one difference of opinion would cost them dearly.

'Heads!' called Arnold as Arthur flipped the coin high into the night air.

The penny coin seemed to hang for several long seconds before being caught by the boy's gloved hand. Arthur peeked at the coin, King George V's head staring back at him.

'Tough!' Arthur said quickly returning the coin to his pocket.

Arnold groaned, pulled a silly face and that was that.

The twins stayed to shelter beneath the tree but only the boy in the black balaclava and gloves knew the truth. Arnold had really won the toss and they should have been racing one another home. Each would have trusted the other with their life. They didn't know it but they just had. Shadow began to whine and nuzzle up close to the boys. Arthur bent down with comforting arms.

'There, you're all right. We'll look after you,' he said lovingly stroking Shadow's wet fur and hugging the dog whose front legs were trembling.

Every rumble of thunder out-boomed the last. It was as if the Giant Colossus of Ancient Rhodes had come alive and was walking ever closer towards them. Shadow whimpered, his front legs trembling even more, not wanting to sit and nudging the boys for attention. Shadow wanted to go and tugged on his lead. Suddenly a fork of lightning speared the darkness. The night sky flicker flashed once more followed by one almighty thunderous boom. At this moment, Nature used its power with devastating results. The oak tree was struck by lightning and so too were the two sheltering children. Seconds later the tree was ablaze and one of its hefty branches hit Arthur before crashing to the ground and trapping him unconscious beneath it. However, that wasn't all. A mysterious swirling mist whipped up Arnold's crumpled body and took it away into the cold night air. Nobody else had witnessed what seemed to be more like a supernatural force rather than Nature's wrath itself. Whatever it was, it carried the child like a flimsy rag doll higher and higher into the stormy sky.

The scorched ground and the stricken oak tree later became an unmarked memorial to the tragedy. That night had been 'the last time, the last goodbye,' just the boys hadn't known it.

On stormy nights, some still claimed they heard a child's sobs carried on the wind. Others said that it was the stuff of fanciful minds, an overactive imagination and that that was all. Nobody in the village would ever forget that ill-fated night when Nature chose to use its weapons of destruction to punish them. It was a tragedy casting a huge cloud over the village but for one family it had a silver lining.

Chapter 2

HEAVENLY GARDENS

Whoever first said that time is a healer, lied. It is not, not really. People say it to make tough, sad stuff a bit better. When tragedy strikes, the heart aches, really aches. It hangs heavy like a sodden blanket weighing you down, and yet the sun still shines, rising and setting without the world so much as blinking. It really sucks that nothing feels your pain. You notice how much people moan about silly stuff as if it were life or death. What really matters if the bus is ten minutes late two days running, or the price of a sliced loaf has gone up a couple of pence? Why do we sweat the small stuff? It is a loss of perspective but it is a very human thing. It stinks that life goes on without any respect for your grief, but it does. This village was no exception although nothing would ever be the same.

Almost fifty years on times had changed and yet the never to be forgotten tragedy was still guarded by the locals like a jackpot winning lottery ticket. According to popular rumour those who had told the tale had fallen victim to a killer curse. Nine men and three gossipy old women had met a sticky end, struck down, one by one, in a series of unexplained incidents. The most recent, some eighteen months earlier, was a dentist with a dislike of hard-boiled sweets who had choked to death on a peppermint flavoured 'Bulls Eye.' It had happened only hours after mocking the curse and its story. There were no suspicious circumstances, nobody else involved; everyone knew that it was the dreaded deadly 'C-U-R-S-E'. Nevertheless, newcomers still came to settle in this village of whispers. The Tipples were one such family who almost half a century after the incident had occurred, were to find their own lives touched by it.

Things were very different back then. The 'Seventies' was a decade of grit and glamour, a time of simple pleasures and complicated formality. Adults were addressed as 'Mr. This' or 'Mrs. That', 'Sir' or 'Madam,' a first name used only for a person near the top of your Christmas card list. There were no mobile phones, home computers or social media. Digital photography was not a thing either; photographers, like you and me, requiring a film and a large amount of patience, waiting often months to finish the film before a further delay whilst it was being processed. There was no delete button either, you got what you shot. Televisions were still mainly black and white, bulky units, often called 'the box' with only three channels and no remote controls or ways of recording. If you missed it, you missed it! Men ruled the work place and women, the kitchen sink, although 'Women's Lib.' had found its voice and was about to shake things up. On a purely human level, being different in any way was seldom understood or tolerated. Life was unfair, unkind and generally unchallenged. This was a country in crisis with shortages of stuff like sugar and toilet rolls and an economy saddled with a thing called 'galloping inflation' that turned out to be nothing to do with horses at all! It meant that there were daily price rises on everything you bought and together with work strikes, power cuts and candles it made for a challenging time.

It was the very hot summer of 1976. The sun was high in the sky as three children laden down with school clobber were completing their mile long journey back from school. The parched, flat countryside had changed from green to brown and as they marched along in the sweltering heat, they chanted like well-drilled army recruits on a boot camp exercise.

'We are Tipples 1, 2, 3,

Alex, Tiggy and Penelope.

Right, left, right, left, right.
We go to school and work hard, too,
We are Tipples through and through.'

The youngest was Tiggy. On her birth certificate she was Tina, but by four years of age, she had rejected the name outright and put her hands over her ears if anyone called her by it. 'Tiggy', as she preferred, looked like a girl right enough but walked like a boy. She had the shoulder rolling, springy swagger of a lad who fancies himself as a bit of a hotshot footballer. Her long, dark hair was in a messy ponytail and a candy cigarette lodged on the top of her ear. Tiggy loved to copy 'ace stuff' as she called it, and had seen the man who worked in the village shop do it with real cigarettes. She prodded her shoe into the back of her brother's knee and giggled as his leg collapsed. Alex was the oldest but was used to it and began to pick up the scattered books and papers he had dropped on the dusty ground.

'Wespect!' said the boy, failing to roll his 'r's' in his usual manner, and offering his sister a friendly clash of fists.

Suddenly from out of the blue, speeding like a homicidal maniac, appeared a scruffy looking lad on a Chopper (a bicycle with high-rise handlebars and high-back seat which was the 'must have' item for seventies coolness) with a bulgy eyed boy holding on for dear life behind.

'Watch out, it's Mikey and Toadie!' said Alex. 'You do wealise Mikey fancies you, Pen, it's scwibbled in felt pen on all the lavatowy walls. I twied to remove it with a damp sheet of Izal but it didn't shift with even the world's scwatchiest loo paper.'

Penelope, the middle child, died a little behind her long, brown hair as the cyclist approached. Mikey's school shirt, covered in 'Leaver's Day' felt tip, was unbuttoned to his sun burnt waist whilst on his head was a pair of not so white Y fronts. The boy gobbed out a pink gummy globule and then rooted up his nostrils with his grubby fingers, flicking the rich pickings at Alex.

'Here! Professor Tips! Have one of my glow-in-the-dark bogies…. call it a souvenir!' Mikey shouted hurtling his wheels over an exercise book and wolf whistling at Penelope.

Toadie spat and burped and then they were gone as quickly as they had appeared. Penelope, the eldest of the two girls, squirmed.

'They don't call him Mikey Mucus for nothing!' Tiggy said half disgusted and amused.

'I just wish he took his weputation less sewiously,' grumbled Alex picking up the last of the books.

'Can't wait to ride my BMX!' said Tiggy, her golden green cat-like eyes sparkling.

'I haven't seen Mrs.D for ages.'

Penelope looked anxious.

'Don't upset them! Mum hates that bike and the stuff you do on it,' she said. 'And no pestering to get the brakes removed again. You know she goes nuts!'

'That blinking bike is more taboo than Germaine Gweer burning her bwa,' teased Alex. 'She thinks it makes you like a boy.'

'She's hinting for us to take up knitting!' said Penelope.

Tiggy burst out laughing.

'Me knit? Don't be daft!' responded Tiggy kicking a stone in frustration. 'You're always crazing for a dog. I reckon that probably gets on her wick more! Even if they think me doing tricks on my bike isn't a girl thing, they can't stop me!' She kicked up a few more stones and a load of dust in defiance.

The children rounded the corner out of the countryside into the brick-weave grandeur of Heavenly Gardens. They immediately fell silent passing the grand ornamental lions at the entrance of the first driveway. Nobody said another word until arriving home to Number 6, Pearly Gates, whose clean white railings glinted in the summer sunshine.

Number 6 was like a huge dolls' house with a lawn like a bowling green. It was so perfectly neat that it seemed a crime to walk on it. The large garden boasted lots of rose arches whilst the house and its perfect paintwork had so many bedrooms that even Mr. and Mrs. Tipple had one each. The close itself was Union Jack land and stone statues and fountains popped up everywhere. The rest of Great Snubington was very different to Heavenly Gardens, known in the village as the place where 'The Poshies lived.' To The Tipples, Pearly Gates was their dream home on a dream close.

The children got on well and were very close in age too, having been a clean sweep of premature births. Alex loved the jeopardy of it all. He wanted the world to know what 'miwacles' they were to have survived and always insisted upon quoting their ages in days. Alexander (a.k.a 'Confucius' on account of his worldly wisdom), had clocked up 4,340 days, making him almost twelve, Penelope had just turned 11 having tallied 4,017 days and the youngest, Tiggy at 3,613 days, was making plans for her 10th birthday. She was a cheeky, fun-loving, fidgeting ball of fire who just could not keep still. Small as a pixie but a giant in impact, her smile and dimpled cheeks were like a magic light wherever she went. Alex described his little sister as 'a unicorn in a field of horses.' Most families have a 'naughty one' and Tiggy was theirs. Add to the mix a creative streak, it made for a lethal combination. In fact, it had changed the family history when she dressed up the soft toys in her mother's underwear and paraded them on their street. A camel wearing her bra on its humps and a gorilla in a Playtex 24–hour girdle (an uncomfortable tummy strangling version of modern day flatteners like Spanx); Alison Tipple could not cope with the humiliation. A fresh start in a new home seemed the only solution and by the end of the year, the family had moved to Heavenly Gardens.

The Tipple children were buzzing. They had waited all year for 'the big one' and now the summer holidays were here, all six weeks of it. Their mother, an attractive woman beneath her frumpy fashion victim outfits, abandoned the roses that she was admiring to greet her own three little rosebuds coming up the driveway. Somewhere in Alison Tipple's jungle of tangled feelings, she was pleased to see them but nobody would have had a clue.

A monstrosity of cartons and toilet roll tubes was sticking out from Tiggy's rucksack. Alison Tipple had an antenna for stuff going indoors and had already spotted it.

'Ta-da! RMS Titanic!' Tiggy announced, yanking it out and squashing it a bit. In fact, quite a big bit.

'There's no room on the mantelpiece! Or anywhere else!' barked her mother, instantly bursting her youngest daughter's bubble.

'Wow, that's weally wadical, Tig....the Titanic after it hit the iceberg....bwilliant!' said Alex, trying to compensate for his mother by pretending to admire the dilapidated model for a solid two minutes.

Thomas Tipple or rather 'Father' as his family called him, including his wife, was a gardening ninja. Nothing disturbed him when he was busy outside. All the same, Penelope, a 'Daddy's Girl' and keen dancer, hovered to catch his eye, practicing some moves whilst she waited but he did not look up and a hundred pirouettes later, her father still had not seen her. Two topiary cockerels stood proud either side of the front door. Tiggy tugged at the neatly clipped leaves.

'Nice bum father!' she yelled spotting her father's corduroy flares sticking out from a bush.

Her mother scowled.

'Bottom!' the woman corrected but Tiggy was already indoors moving a porcelain figurine off its mat on the hall telephone table. She always did it. However, the battered Titanic had inspired Alex to open the history book in his brain.

'Monday 15th Apwil 1912,' he began. 'What a howendous twagedy! So many pewished. Unsinkable! they said and the maiden voyage turns out to be its last! R.M.S Carpathia's Captain Wostwon, R-O-S-T-R-O-N,' said Alex spelling out the name 'was a wescue hewo but out of eight honeymoon couples only two lived to tell the tale. What a waste of a wedding. In fact, what a waste of six weddings!' he said rummaging in his satchel for their school reports.

Three houses along, Harry Dobson appeared on his front step with a cloth. A whippet of a man, popularly known as 'Flash' because of the lightning speed he did things; he polished the brass knocker on his door and disappeared indoors. He did it twice a day every day.

'So how was it?' enquired Alison Tipple brushing away some fuzz balls from some sticky weed on her son's sleeve.

'Pwedictable! The usual leavers' day pwanks,' said Alex rolling his eyes, 'Mikey sneaked wotten eggs into the staff woom and Toadie claimed he had been the victim of an alien abduction duwing bweak time. I know he had an appointment for his bwace, the morwon!'

'Silly boys!' said Alison Tipple 'and the girls?'

'They were kissing everwyone and spweading their germs!' Alex shuddered. 'I put my stewile mask on and hid under the desk,' he said removing it from his pocket to demonstrate.

Up the road, the Gotobeds from Number 21 were returning from a weekly visit to their poodle's psychotherapist. Anybody who was anybody in the village knew the animal's case history. A dog that thought it was a human was always going to be a talking point.

'School weports!' Alex announced, handing his mother three official looking envelopes. 'We had shirt signing. Anyone would think they won't see each other again! In 44 days,' he said checking his digital watch, '17 hours they will all be at the Secondawy Modern. The last time at pwimawy does not mean THE last time at school together. I did twy to tell them but you know how widiculous kids are! Thank heavens for Gwammar School and the 11+ and me being the only one to pass.'

Alison Tipple scanned her son's immaculate snowy white shirt and looked relieved.

'The ink would never have come out in the wash,' she mumbled as Alex walked away unaware that his shorts flies were undone.

The school reports, like the children, were very different. Penelope's was glowing. The sort that might make other kids parents' sick. You know the tiger type with a competitive nature that does their kid's homework for them and wants their child to be recognised as the smartest. Tiggy's report on the other hand, made her mother look as if she had just stood in dogs' poo in her most prestigious shoes. Schoolwork was mostly a mystery to her, although she was a wiz at arty stuff. She was a right fidget pants too and almost anything was more interesting than the actual teacher's lesson. Tiggy could tell you if there was an insect on the floor, what was in the bin, the number of cars that had passed the window and the colour of the teacher's socks. It was quite a skill really. Admittedly, not the right skill for a parent who wants to brag about their kid's school report. Fortunately, Alex's report was so superhumanly impressive that Alison Tipple thought she had given birth to a genius.

'Guess who?' boomed Tiggy creeping up behind and placing her hands over her mother's eyes that were re-reading Alex's report for the third time.

Alison Tipple threw them aside. Not put off, Tiggy squeezed the ice block around her waist. Her mother recoiled from the public display of affection. The Riches' eldest boy, down the road playing a very good 'keepy downy' version of 'keepy uppy' with his new football, neither noticed nor could have cared less. Tiggy stooped down, picking a rare daisy from the lawn and handed it to her mother with a huge smile. Alison Tipple stood like stone.

'You're an embarrassment! We've tried so hard to fit in here, except for you and that wretched bike! I've bought that many pairs of shoes to please them but now this!' said Alison Tipple waving Tiggy's report and turning red in the face. 'News like this travels fast. Before you know it, they'll all know!' Having spotted two of the residents appearing in the distance up the road she lowered her voice to a menacing whisper. 'Why, oh why can't you be like your brother and sister? You always have to let us down,' the woman chided, crushing the daisy. ' Boy first, and then a girl. Perfect! Whatever were we thinking!' she muttered but it was still loud enough for Tiggy to hear. Alison Tipple threw the daisy to the ground and did one of her 'super flounces' into the house.

Tiggy crumbled inside, the words piercing like a dagger into her heart. She always felt the odd one out. Penelope, who had been within earshot posed in an arabesque, swooped in, picked up the daisy and wrapped her arms like a cotton wool blanket around her sister. They both knew a punishment was coming.

Chapter 3

PEARLY GATES

'Aaaagh greenfly!' yelled Father. They've decimated the Fun Day lupins!'

Thomas Tipple held his head in his hands, pacing the flowerbeds, inspecting the damage.

'That's it! I give up! I'll never grow another lupin as long as I live!'

Thomas Tipple's despair had woken the Gotobeds' dog asleep in the garden hammock whilst several 'concerned' residents, who in reality just loved a good 'nose,' had loitered in their gardens watching the drama unfold. With so many flowers at risk, the whole family pitched in. Thomas Tipple had declared war on the 'little blighters.'

'I'm done with lupins! I'm going to job the job and save the rest!' he said checking his other flowers for green fly.

'Ex-ter-min-ate! Ex-ter-min-ate!' Alex ordered, looking and sounding like a dalek as he joined in, his forearms held rigidly in front of him whilst spraying insecticide all over the place. Soon there were dead bodies everywhere but it was at a price.

'I've ruined my French manicure!' gasped Alison Tipple, looking with regret at her nails.

'And I reek of insecticide!' said Penelope passing her mother a nail file out of the 'Odds and Ends' drawer.

Alex was sneezing. It was the pollen but he loved the drama of it being from getting so many bugs up his nose.

'This has to be the longest sneezing fit in the histowy of the universe,' he boasted checking in his Guinness Book of Records and sneezing again.

Nevertheless, by the time that the youngest Tipple had got back from taking a package from a home catalogue order to the outskirts of the village, apart from Alex's chronic sneezing fit, it seemed just like any other day.

On her way in, Tiggy plucked a few leaves from the topiary cockerels' combs because their neatness annoyed her. Her mother was in the kitchen savagely beating up eggs with a fork, her bottom wobbling in her new midi skirt like a sumo wrestler sprinting for sushi. Penelope was soaking her smelly insecticide hands in a bowl of soapy water. The gymnastics at the

Montreal Olympics was on the kitchen's black and white television and Penelope, watched spellbound, her fingers becoming more and more prune-like with every gymnast's routine. Alex was pacing the Flotex flooring in a tail coated dinner jacket and bow tie with a brand new Queen's Silver Jubilee tea towel draped over his arm, apparently on 'butler duty.' However, he had to be the noisiest butler ever, laying the table and singing David Bowie's 'Star Man' in between sneezes. Apart from the pair of yellow flippers he was wearing unable to find his slippers, everything was as expected.

Meal times at the Tipples were family fixtures that mattered. 'A family that eats together, stays together' was the family motto. Pearly Gates smelt of bleach and beeswax but the scent of polish was at its strongest in the dining room. The furniture had extra shiny surfaces and the sparkle of finely cut crystal attacked the eyeballs from every angle. A pattern called 'Floral Fantasy' was Alison Tipple's bid for a bit of swag and designer flair, appearing on curtains, wall clock, plates, knives and forks alike.

'We're the third home to own a colour television, and now we're even all matching in the dining room. We really are starting to fit in here!' said Alison Tipple stroking her curtains and feeling a bit posh.

Tiggy had hoped the stress of the aphid attack might have made her parents forget about her lousy report.

Alex, who having removed his tailcoat was now off duty as a butler, had switched back to 'clever Alex' mode and almost distracted them at the meal table.

'Father, don't wowwy about another aphid attack! I've been weading all about their life cycle and I think I may have the solution,' said Alex taking a piece of paper from his tie-dyed shirt pocket. 'Aphis gossypii Glover, the common aphid to you,' he looked around the table at everyone, 'need not be a thweat to your plants, Father.' He paused, 'Wepwoduction…'

Alison Tipple blushed, a rash appearing like a violent allergic reaction on her neck. Tiggy giggled sensing Alex had said a naughty word.

'We just have to stop them wepwoducing. That means no se…'

Alison Tipple fake coughed to divert from the conversation.

'We've a school report and punishment to discuss. Isn't that right Father?' she said, elbowing her husband so sharply in the ribs that he winced. 'I really can't imagine why you are finding this all so funny!' She glared at her youngest daughter who was still grinning.

Tiggy's biggest dread was a grounding and ban on her BMX. Anything else she could cope with. Biking was her world: the one thing that gave her life. Her mother described the bike as being her youngest daughter's favourite 'waste of time,' but it was Tiggy's light out of the Greygoyle darkness and for which, she also happened to have an undeniable talent.

Fortunately, 'Father' with his more tolerant view of girls on bikes meant her BMX riding was safe. Extra chores and school 'catch-up' lessons from Alex was, she felt, a good result.

'No wowwies Tig we'll have a wight laugh!' whispered Alex into her ear. 'I've got some Opal Fruits!'

Her brother was like a walking Wikipedia. Any topic from 'The Big Bang' to the Orangutan, Alex had the facts however random. He even spiced up the dull stuff. Put simply, Alex made geeky, cool.

Two hours later, the lupins were burning in the garden incinerator and Tiggy had completed her chores for the day. She rolled her bell-bottom trousers up to the knees securing them with an elastic band, always the sign that she was off biking. A huge buddleia bush was the gatekeeper to her BMX. It stood like a sprawling leafy giant guarding the entry to the potting shed and more importantly, obstructed the view of the back of the shed where Tiggy kept her second-hand BMX, her pride and joy. Parked beneath a waterproof sheet behind the buddleia, behind the shed nobody would have known it was there. She hoped to see some butterflies on the buddleia's earliest blooms but there were none and her father was not even to blame. Butterflies were fine but he hated slugs and so, Tiggy's two pet slugs, 'Sluggy' and 'Huggy,' remained a closely guarded secret, living behind the shed beneath some rotting wood. Bike rides were the perfect excuse to visit them and well aware her father was a bug-busting, slug-slaying fiend, Tiggy was always relieved to find the two slugs alive.

'Slugs are pests!' Thomas Tipple said almost every day. 'I pity any slug stupid enough to come into my garden!'

Tiggy didn't dare spend long behind the shed because her mother was like a secret agent and detective rolled into one and was in prime spying position, cutting flowers in the prettiest border for the following days Residents Watch meeting.

'You'll need a shed load if The Stink Potters are coming!' cheeked Tiggy wheeling past her bicycle and handing her mother a checklist of her completed jobs. 'Her nasty Avon perfume and his cheesy feet!' she said screwing up her nose. 'Alex says they could fell a giant at ten paces. No wonder their cat left home!'

Secretly, Alison Tipple agreed but scowled anyway. She had been dreading her turn at hosting and falling short of the residents high standards. Extra air fresheners should deal with the smelly couple and honing in her glare onto the bike she watched her daughter disappear around the corner.

Thomas Tipple's car was spotless. It was always

spotless. This man lived to work and was in the driveway buffing up his Hillman Avenger as if his life depended upon it. As she passed, Tiggy could see her reflection in the bodywork and twanging on her father's braces she speeded away. Thomas Tipple, so focused on his handiwork, was unsure of quite what had happened.

'That's another job jobbed,' he said under his breath as he realigned his braces and straightened his belt.

Chapter 4

THE LIGHTNING TREE

The woods were a frog's leap from Heavenly Gardens. They belonged to a wonderful farmer's widow called Mrs. Derbyshire, but to Tiggy, she was her 'Mrs.D' She was an open-minded, fun-loving 70 year old and had invited the Tipple children to visit for 'whatever, whenever' they liked.

'My only rule is that you let your hair down and enjoy yourselves!' Mrs. Derbyshire said whenever she saw them.

In stark contrast, Heavenly Gardens had hundreds of rules, 'Do's and Don'ts' and banned stuff, including cars old enough to be considered 'old bangers,' shirts not tucked into trousers, chewing gum, ball games and space hoppers. Bikes were not popular either, unless it was brand new and had a basket on the front. Tiggy's love of adventure and BMXing meant Mrs. Derbyshire had given her young friend the greatest gift of all....the very means to be free.

A tiny gap in the hedge was the doorway to this new and exciting world. From here, a narrow track, only ever used by the Tipples, led to one of nature's secrets. A tranquil, unspoiled wilderness of zesty scents and flower splashed meadows melted into a wooded horizon. Close up, bobble-headed grasses jiggled on the breeze, black-eyed poppies, cornflowers and daisies joining the dance for the perfect country mix. It was a dreamy scene and whatever the weather, Tiggy loved it here. This was an explorer's paradise. The long sunny spell had baked cracks into the dusty track that weaved through the meadows as far as a whitewashed stone farmhouse and it was here that Mrs. Derbyshire lived.

The house nestled amongst a tangle of bushes that had run riot since Mr. Derbyshire's death, whilst in the background a windmill with battered sails added extra charm. It was like a scene on a fancy chocolate box lid, the sort that you keep stuff in long after the goodies are gone and Alison Tipple, who had recently been attending the village art classes, considered it the perfect subject for her entry for the forthcoming Fun Day art competition. How Tiggy loved the feeling of freedom as she left The Close behind!

Tiggy biked past the windows inwardly celebrating

her escape. There was always somebody watching from somewhere and today was no exception. The two men from Number 11, one of them still in his tartan bathrobe, were in a smoochy embrace in their porch. It was 1976 and seeing Tiggy, they swiftly parted.

Hidden from view and yet a mere stone's throw from her home, Mrs. Derbyshire's and 'Pearly Gates' were in all other ways worlds apart. Once there, Tiggy changed. It was like an explosion of energy, a fusion of power and skill as she burst into action, her long tawny hair full of tomboy tangles streaming out behind her. She was fierce and fearless, racing along the track, riding the bumps like an expert skier negotiating a mogul field until further along several abandoned straw bales made an inviting launch pad impossible for her to resist. A rabbit scurried for cover beneath the nearest bramble bush, only the disturbed clouds of dust daring to get in her way.

It was not long before Tiggy came to a tree known by the oldest inhabitants of the village as 'The Lightning Tree.' It was, in fact, the very same tree that almost fifty years earlier had been the tragic spot the twin brothers, on the eve of their 10th birthday, had fallen victim to the storm. These days, apart from Tiggy, who would often stop for a drink here, only the magpies visited. It was all a bit sinister seeing the jagged boughs and the bird's black feathers and beady eyes staring at her. In fact, they freaked her out and made her tummy wobble, and so to keep in their good books she would always salute them, regardless of the time of day.

'Good afternoon, Mr. Magpie!' she said and then usually they would fly away.

Today the sun was bright in the sky and the tree's stunted trunk and gnarled naked branches cast eerie shadows across the farmland. A robin was pecking about at the base of the trunk but the magpies disappeared as soon as they saw her and seeing them gone, Tiggy stopped to read the many messages carved into its bleached, bark-bare trunk. She knew them all inside out and as she ran her fingers over the rough edges of a crudely cut heart, Tiggy chewed on a piece of Juicy Fruit gum, her favourite biking staple.

'A.R. 12/11/28, 'A R & JD TRUE LOVE', 'JD4AR,' she read aloud tracing the initials with her finger and enthusiastically chewing out the gum's flavour before moulding it with her tongue to make a new monster. At first, it didn't seem any different to her previous time outs at the tree, but it was. The wind was getting up. What had been just a gentle breeze cooling her hot skin was now like a tiger roaring, whipping up the dirt and flattening the long grass at the sides of the track. The fierce force of the wind scrambled her hair and as it beat into her face, the wind's wildness was a refreshing assault to her sweat-beaded brow.

The church bells, some distance away, were ringing like a backing track to the wind. She thought it was probably a bell-ringing practise for the Fun Day in a few days' time. The dirt was still swirling like a desert sand storm and the ground that had been undisturbed in years was suddenly exposed. Tiggy bent down; an old penny coin had been unearthed. She had never seen one like it before. It was large, and made of copper that was now so dark and discoloured that it was almost black. On the 'heads' side it had a man with a grand moustache and on 'tails' a woman with a helmet and a shield. Alex could have told her that they were King George V and Britannia 'who ruled the waves,' but she had no idea who they were. Hoping to find a few more coins, Tiggy scuffed her feet over the ground. The robin had joined her and seemed to be looking, too, but there were no more pennies, just an old firework shell, its writing faint and faded. She stared at the hollow tube, making out the letters 'C-A-N-D' when the chilling chant of a young child came from the direction of the tree, very possibly from the carvings. The chant was familiar to Tiggy but not the voice. It definitely sounded like a boy and it was the song that Mrs. Derbyshire used to sing to her whenever the old lady had said that it was 'raining cats and dogs' outside:

'It's raining, it's pouring, the old man is snoring,' Tiggy snatched back her hand as if the tree was on fire and the singing instantly stopped.

'That's my monster's tail gone!' she muttered, the shock causing her accidentally to swallow the last of her gum.

Tiggy stared at the spot from where the voice had come from, but now there was nothing to see or hear. The robin was watching though, despite the wind still whistling and howling. She removed a fresh piece of gum from its foil and dared her finger back to the carvings. A little bit of her wanted to hear the voice again but a big bit hoped not to because it was so creepy. Her finger quivered over the carvings and began tracing the letter A, and as if it was a switch, the child's voice immediately returned. This time it was louder and even more chilling and when the song came to its familiar ending, the singing turned to sobs as if upset that the old man 'couldn't get up in the morning.' Tiggy liked a good mystery to solve, but this was no ordinary mystery like who took the last chocolate, or who squeezed the toothpaste tube in the middle...this was scary. Everyone knew that the village had a curse and over the years, twelve people had died in mysterious ways. Tiggy knew this too, but had no idea that this stricken oak tree was the famed 'Lightning Tree' and was a tree with a grisly story to tell.

Subsequently, Tiggy referred to this episode as 'The Spooky Secret,' only sharing it with 'Pirate Pants' her

'Go everywhere bear,' that she would never leave home without.

'It has to be our secret or we'll never be allowed here again!' she said wagging a finger at the well-loved, balding, cuddly toy. 'And without Mrs.D.'s there's no biking.'

Tiggy knew that with anything odd the villagers and her parents got jumpy and usually because of the dreaded killer C-U-R-S-E. However, what happened next all happened so quickly that she had no time to think about curses or anything else as a sudden gust of wind blew Tiggy backwards, nearly knocking her off her feet. A bleached, bark bare branch crashed to the ground, narrowly missing both Tiggy and her bike that was lying at the foot of the tree. She inspected her BMX, giving the handlebars a full 360 degrees rotation and seeing the bars move freely Tiggy was pleased that her newly-fitted brake cable 'detangler' had not come to any harm. She mounted her bike, feeling for the pedals and as soon as her feet touched them, the wind suddenly died down, the dirt settled, the church bells stopped ringing and even the robin had flown away. It had all been most unexpected and, in a way, thrilling but Tiggy was happy to have left the tree and the weird goings on behind.

Cycling on and many stops and bike tricks later, Mrs. Derbyshire's farmhouse was on her stomach's radar. 'Mrs.D' was a great baker of cakes. It was never anything that fancy but it tasted amazing and Tiggy always loved, as she called it, to 'stuff her face' there. The very thought made Tiggy's legs pump even harder. The farm gate was open as usual and rocketing through it on one wheel, she skidded to a halt.

Mrs. Derbyshire was like the perfect Gran except she had no children. Instead, she kept chickens, a black pot-bellied pig called Churchill, and a naughty donkey named 'Don Quixote' who had once eaten a pair of slippers. Add to this the 'Dolly Mixtures', a mix of three different breeds of sheep and two dewy-eyed Jersey cows, Patrick and Patricia, fondly known as the 'Cow Pats' it was a motley and interesting crew. There was certainly nothing grand or flash about Mrs. Derbyshire or her home. She was somebody who very much understood the value of things rather than the price. Her only fashion statement was in the type of apron (she called it her 'pinny') she wore to cheer up the drabness of her housekeeper's overall.

'I can't be doing with fashion fads. I like what I like! As long as it keeps my clothes clean, it will do!'

Mrs. Derbyshire said about the shapeless nylon garment. She always wore one despite her stiff joints struggling with the buttons that fastened all the way up the front.

Tiggy's characteristic six rap rhythmical knock

brought Mrs.D bustling to the door, her full moon rosy-cheeked face crinkling with delight at the sight of her young friend wiping her feet on the doormat.

'Well, if it isn't my Little Special!' she greeted her, brushing off her floury hands onto the front of her apron. She wrapped her arms tightly around the child and squeezed her almost breathless into her layers of comfortable plumpness. Tiggy had always squirmed at the sight of the hairs sprouting from the local 'Bitch Queen's' mole. However, the odd grey whisker on Mrs.D's double chin went unnoticed, consumed by her warmth and kindness. Tiggy felt like she mattered more than anyone in the world.

'Come on in, Treasure!' she said trying not to show her teeth as she smiled.

In all honesty, Mrs. Derbyshire's teeth were awful! They were dreadfully crooked with one badly chipped from slipping on the ice during 'The Big Freeze' of 1963, but usually, her teeth never remained hidden for very long.

'Don't you go looking at my teeth!' she would say wagging her finger playfully at Tiggy. 'You will be having nightmares!' and then she would ruin it all by laughing so heartily that her teeth showed even more!

To Tiggy, her smile was instant central heating for her heart. Whatever her problem or worries Mrs.D made her better, although she would have said it was the other way round. However, today her smile was almost a bit feeble, her teeth did not show at all.

'Ahh! Miss Tigs, my little ray of sunshine! Even on such a sad day as this. Dear Mr. Dodds! I just can't quite believe it!'

Tiggy shrugged her shoulders. All she knew was that Mr. Dodds went to church, and was a door to door sales representative for Kleeneze and was often at their front door dressed in a pin stripe suit talking to her mother.

'You mean Mr. Dodds, the churchy one?' she said taking the sherbet fountain that Mrs.D was teasing into her hand.

'That's right, Miss Tigs. He rings the bells. Rather, he did ring the bells. Mrs.D's eyes were filling with tears and her front chin was starting to quiver. 'The poor man got snagged to the bell rope and couldn't release himself. He fell from the bell tower just this afternoon when he was practicing with my friend, Dolly,' she said shaking her head. 'That ol' Fun Day has got a lot to answer for.'

Tiggy's eyes were on stalks.

'Tangled up he was!' said Mrs.D removing a handkerchief from her overall pocket and sniffling into it. 'Such a lovely, lovely man. He used to play dominoes with my Charlie back in the day. The last time I saw him I had a bug and made my excuses not to hang around. Makes me feel awful rushing off like that but I didn't know it was the last time I'd ever see him.' She let out a little sob, quickly muffling it for her visitor's sake.

'I didn't hear an ambulance, just bells,' said Tiggy nibbling the liquorice sticking out from the sherbet fountain's yellowy cardboard tube that Mrs.D had slipped into her hand.

'He went up and down with the bell 'til he dropped. I just came off the phone to Dolly. She saw it happen and said nobody could do anything to save him. There wasn't time for an ambulance.'

'I'll tell Mum,' Tiggy said feeling sad that Mrs.D looked upset.

'They're saying it's that wicked old curse to blame. Perhaps best not to tell her or talk about it. I'll give your Mum a ring because she will want to know,' Mrs.D said dabbing her eyes with her handkerchief.

The birds were singing when Tiggy went on her way again. She rode along counting butterflies and swigging squash from a bottle until she arrived at a derelict windmill. It stood like a wounded Amazonian angel against the skyline, dominating the landscape with a rural charm that was even more striking because of its ragged sails. Tiggy often hung out here, chalking graffiti onto the curvy walls (Mrs. Derbyshire didn't mind) and with Pants, her constant companion, she visualised herself biking her way to glory. On her last visit, she had drawn a huge picture of herself wearing a medal, coloured in with yellow chalk, forgetful her parents dismissed her gold medal dreams as 'unrealistic nonsense.' Here, it did not matter if she behaved like a boy or a girl, what she did or planned to do. She was just plain old Tiggy who loved to do tricks on a bike. Since breaking up from school, Penelope and Tiggy had binge watched the television coverage of The Olympics, mesmerised by the talent of Romanian gymnast, Nadia Comaneci. For the first time in the history of the sport, the tiny gymnast had achieved the perfect score. The facts were that Nadia was a small, fourteen-year-old girl who had taken the world by storm. What more proof, Tiggy asked herself, could anyone want that age and gender were no barrier to skill, strength or anything.

'You're the only one who really gets me,' Tiggy whispered to Pants. 'You know all my secrets, even the baddest!' she said adjusting the panda's patch so that it completely covered its missing eye. 'If you've watched the telly and seen a human walking on the Moon like Mum and Father have, why on earth would you think anything was impossible?'

Stuff always made sense here and found its natural order.

'The girls are coming Pants! I'll prove them wrong!' Tiggy told her bear.

Things were continuing to be a bit strange today though. A large puddle was seeping from the back of the ivy-covered mill. There had been no rain in weeks and the serious water shortage had meant that a hosepipe ban was in force. She carefully picked her way, looking at her reflection in the clear water that glistened in the sunshine.

'The Boggle. You've done this!' she mumbled staring at an old wooden barrel stood at the puddle's edge.

It had been a fixture there for as long as she could remember and the late Mr. Derbyshire had told her many stories about 'The Boggle that lived in a barrel.' They had all started the same way and looking at it, she could hear him now.

'Once upon a time when the pigs drank wine and the monkeys smoked tobacco there lived a Boggle....'

Apparently, 'The Boggle' was friendly, never washed behind its floppy ears and was scared of the Bogey Man. Tiggy often bombarded Mr. Derbyshire with questions about the monster.

'What about greens, like sprouts and cabbage? Would he eat them?' Tiggy wanted to know because she hated them.

'Good gracious no!' Mr. Derbyshire had replied. 'He only eats sky-blue pink pie in the sky washed down with ginger beer!'

Nevertheless, The Boggle was magic and could

do anything, so what was a puddle in a drought! Oddly enough, the windmill door was also peeping open. Tiggy clung on to Pants for comfort and poked open the rickety door. A barn owl, woken up by the sudden noise and brightness, flew straight towards her, its magnificent wings skimming her head before it disappeared into the daylight. Tiggy smirked, sighing with relief as she closed the door firmly shut again.

The day had certainly got off to a bit of a weird start. Tiggy took out a lemon from the pouch of her kangaroo top to begin on her 'Big list of silly skills.' Sucking on a lemon was a new entry and was worth 2 'Skillage' points. 'Sucking on a lemon without pulling a face' was worth 3 points. She hurtled past the old abandoned tractor, covered in the snowy deposits of visiting birds. It had done its final day's work on the same sad day that Mr. Derbyshire had also worked his last. Mrs. Derbyshire had insisted the tractor should stay there.

The day had dawned pink with a golden promise of sunshine. By late afternoon, it was still so hot and sticky that Tiggy was pleased to reach the shaded wood. It was a favourite spot for her tricks. The light was soft and dappled, the shafts filtering through the trees, painting its mystical beams upon the undergrowth as if a spaceship was about to land. The foxglove glade was losing its colour. Last month it had been awash with crimson and buttermilk spires, and buzzing busily with bulbous-bodied bees. Nevertheless, the log piles and mossy mounds were ideal for Tiggy to perfect her skills. She had had several failed attempts at a host of new tricks, including the Superman. Right now, it wasn't happening, she couldn't do it. It had to be just a blip. Time and effort was all it needed because she was like a magician on her bike and she knew she could make it do anything. From one log pile to another, Tiggy sailed through the air, the whites of her eyes bulging wide as she spotted her landing. She made it look so easy, her body perfectly poised and streamlined, the bike surrendering to her supreme control. Suddenly, a pheasant was disturbed in the undergrowth. A child's figure was wading through the chest-high bracken....a boy...in Mrs. Derbyshire's wood where nobody but the Tipples ever ventured. However, in a flash he was gone.

Chapter 5

THE GREYGOYLES

At 10 o'clock the aroma of freshly brewed coffee was wafting through Pearly Gates. Breakfast coffee had been supermarket 'instant' but only the finest coffee beans would do for The Residents Watch. Alison Tipple was nervous. She had one final check of the living room, hiding her knitting bag behind the sofa. Her 'Home Makers' Weekly' on the coffee table had fallen victim to Tiggy's new felt tip pens. The cover model now had spots, black teeth, a beard and other hairy bits. Alison Tipple had wanted to swap one of its recipes at the end of the meeting but seeing a guest already coming up the drive, in her panic, she tucked it behind a cushion. She felt sick to be hosting the meeting and had always managed to dodge doing it in the past; however, there are only so many excuses and it had got awkward. This was it. Alison Tipple was beyond the point of no return and with her guests about to arrive the place was set to impress. She took a few deep breaths.

There were always a few apologies for absence, although never from the Luvvies at Number 9 and the Tipples' neighbours, Arthur and Gracie Ramsbottom. They had no desire to be there and were certainly not in the least bit sorry about it! These meetings always attracted the same predictable faces and shiny shoes. Tiggy called them 'The Greygoyles.' In her opinion, they had to be the most boring people on the planet. Grey in every way, they could strangle life with a look and only their painfully dull conversation was more deadly.

Alicia Duncan Forbes, who many of the long-standing villagers referred to as 'The Bitch Queen,' was the first to arrive. She was a rude, nasty human being and a walking designer label. She used the number of zeroes on the end of a number to decide a thing or a person's worth. Her lips without lipstick were invisible and her face and neck had a generous peppering of moles that with age had grown extra wobbly bits. There was one in particular on her chin, which Alicia Duncan Forbes boasted was her 'beauty spot.' It looked like a chocolate drop with hairs sprouting out. Tiggy always counted them. This was her first proper visit to Pearly Gates and so, Alicia Duncan Forbes wishing to look the undisputed 'Queen of Bling,' was wearing what looked like the entire contents of a jewellery box as she jingle-jangled her way into the living room. As usual, she was a 'Lone Ranger,' her current husband (number 4) having so called 'better things to do,'(but everyone knew that he was usually up to no good with another woman) and so her jewellery was her 'plus one.' In fact, her massive one carat diamond ring, known to everyone as 'Mrs. Duncan Forbes' rock,' went with her everywhere, always announced by her little joke.

'It's so funny but I never could stand 'carats' as a child and now I just can't get enough of them!' and she would laugh like a donkey (about her 'carats' not being 'carrots' pun) and the loudest of all.

Emily Gotobed was the next to arrive. She was a terrier of a woman with a nasty temper and arrived wearing a hideous flowery dress and a grimace. Her hairy legs were out on show as usual. They were always the 'elephant in the room' that everyone was aware of but dared not to mention. Her hen-pecked husband was close on her heels, his shoulders stooped and carrying her handbag. Long suffering, Paul Gotobed could never choose his socks of a morning, or have an opinion, and it showed. Tiggy called him 'Old Pug Face.' The poor man had come to repeat everything his wife said and he did not even seem aware of it. The Gotobeds were a peculiar couple, thoroughly miserable together and yet seldom seen apart. They were the furthest pair ever from 'Couples' Goals.' You must have seen their type in the supermarket, bickering as one puts an item in the trolley and the other takes it out!

A further dozen Greygoyles trouped two by two into the Tipples' living room, looking drearier than a wet day at the beach. Greygoyle Man was drab and dapper. It was shoes off, clipboard and pen at the ready. The Grimshaws, Timothy and Gertie were amongst them, the latter carrying a bundle in her arms in a hand knitted blanket. It was her 'baby' but to everyone else it just looked like a garden gnome because that, in fact, is what it was. She wasn't mad, just sad that she had never had any children. Ernest McAvey, a Scotsman to his core, dithered on the doormat to put on his furry plaid slippers and replaced his sandals into his tartan drawstring shoe bag. He always brought it with him along with a packet of shortbread. Terence Tiddy was with him as usual. They adored each other, holding hands when nobody was looking and drawing the same bedroom curtains at night. Their love was obvious, you only had to see how they looked at one another, but it was a time when living a lie was often more acceptable than the truth and so they and everyone else pretended they were 'just friends.'

The priggishly prim 'Greygoyle Ladies,' loved their shoes. Alison Tipple, craving their acceptance, had soon caught the shoe bug, too. Her footwear bill ranked only second to their mortgage but it seemed like a small price to pay to fit in. Surprisingly, Alicia Duncan Forbes was the odd one out since her flat flipper feet were too large for the normal shops.

'Sowwy madam but we sell shoes not canoes,' Alex had jested.

Coffee spoons were tinkling and cups chinking when the doorbell rang. It was the Gibsons from Number 18, standing together in a form of arm lock, wearing matching golf jumpers. In their early thirties, they were the babies of the Greygoyle set but they were so old in their ways that they fitted in like a dream. She called 'tops,' blouses and dresses, 'frocks,' whilst he had never heard of music called 'Punk,' let alone have listened disapprovingly to it.

Tiggy spied from the top of the stairs; the strains of Greygoyle conversation praising the Uppinghams' granddaughters drifted up from below. The oldest, a dental nurse, poured out pink mouth rinse for 'the wealthiest men in the area' whilst the other, a hospital receptionist, not only was invited to the doctors' parties but had 'first refusal' on all the old bed linen as well!

'Ugh! Dead peoples bed sheets. How rank!' muttered Tiggy, bemused that everyone, including her mother, were so impressed.

In Tiggy's mind, these people were ridiculous and

too 'judgy' by half. They hated her BMX and certainly let her know it and were running a 'Stay Home and Knit' Campaign for the Under 12s. They had even hatched a plan to get her started and had put an invitation through the door for Tiggy to join the weekly 'Knit and Natter and Needlepoint Group.' Alex had suggested if it made it more fun, he would learn with her.

'That's no good, you're a boy! We'll then have two problems!' the Greygoyles had responded.

This morning, Tiggy's loathing for them was extra intense and she couldn't bear the prospect of seeing them, despite wanting to hear more about Mr. Dodds. Everyone was still reeling from the news and it was in all the papers. Within 24 hours of the tragedy, word had spread to every corner of the village that the dreaded C-U-R-S-E had struck again. Whether anyone at the meeting would brave bringing it up was another matter.

Not seeing them was worth giving up hearing any curse news and she intended to sneak out undetected, but you know how it is when you are down on your luck, the living room door, typically was peeping open. However, Tiggy's mind was set and she was leaving, no matter what, and having slid all the way to the bottom of the stairs, she was just slinking snake-like through the hall on her belly and privately congratulating herself when the door opened. DUM, DUM, DUM! Timothy Grimshaw on his way out to fetch some postcards from home, towered over her, and the eyes of the entire 'Residents Watch' were burning into her prostrate body on the floor! Alison Tipple looked horrified, as if she was watching puppies drowning, and buried her face inside her coffee cup.

'No offence Mrs. Tipple but (Alison folded her arms in a strong defensive pose waiting for the insult to be unleashed) your youngest is such an odd creature! Are you certain it's not really a boy? On that bike it's definitely more boyish than a boyish boy! Get it knitting and persuade it to grow out of it!' snapped Alicia Duncan Forbes flashing her 'rock' for everyone to see.

'She reminds me so much of the Ramsbottoms' granddaughter,' joined in Mrs. Gibson. 'That one's a bit of a tomboy and wears a cap!' said the woman patting her pageboy hair do. 'Did you see her before she left for the cruise ship?'

Her eyes were transfixed on Alicia Duncan Forbes's ring.

'I saw her!' piped up Hugo F. Uppingham, confident that he was winning in the 'Best Granddaughter' competition, 'Blue hair, studs and wearing one of those disgusting 'Sex Pistols' t-shirts with a safety pin right through Her Majesty!'

'Dreadful!' Mrs. Grimshaw said, still cradling her gnome and rocking it back and forth.

'Disrespectful to our Queen!' berated Hugo F.

Uppingham looking like he had a bad smell under his nose.

'Can you believe the young madam is on a cruise ship being paid to cut peoples hair' said Mrs Gibson, shaking her head and closing her blue eye-shadowed lids to convey her dread.

'You do realise she has a piercing!' Gertie Grimshaw added. 'Punk rocker apparently!'

'Talk about heroes to yobbos in three generations! They need to bring back conscription!' Mr. Grimshaw said with such vigorous disgust he spat a little.

'They need a good hiding!' scolded Mrs. Grimshaw.

'Allow me! I'll gladly do it!' Timothy Grimshaw said drawing attention to the medals on his blazer's lapel that belonged to his late father. Alison Tipple was sufficiently offended to speak up.

'The b----bike is about the only th---thing that they have in c---common,' she stammered, which was something that often happened when under pressure. 'Beverly Ramsbottom gave T-Tiggy her old b- bike so she could v-visit Mrs. D-Derbyshire. You will never s---see my Tiggy with piercings; she would n-never be a p-punk!'

Privately Tiggy had considered this rebellious 'punk craze' to be the bomb and had secretly vowed one day to have a piercing of her very own.

Chapter 6

THE SUNFLOWERS

Darling was the Gotobeds' poodle, and was the only joy in their lives. The couple doted on her. All fluff and bows; she had a different outfit for every day of the week and it was only when Darling refused to go out unless she was wearing Emily Gotobed's jewellery that a psychotherapist was hired. The dog was rumoured to think it was human and so the dressed-up pooch in jewellery and a tutu or leather and tartan, was simply part of the Heavenly Gardens' landscape. The Gotobeds had tied Darling to a lamppost by the entrance to Pearly Gates. Tiggy watched in amusement as the poodle squatted and repeatedly sprayed the post like a leaky hose, thinking how unlike a person Darling could be when it suited.

Next door, Arthur Ramsbottom was steadying himself with his walking stick, his eyes trained on the nesting box that he had put in the cherry tree last winter. A robin was on its little bark roof and he was talking to the bird with the familiarity of an old friend. He had such a positive energy about him that everyone liked Arthur Ramsbottom. Everyone that is, except for The Greygoyles because of his rather bohemian image. They branded him a "hippy" and claimed that at almost sixty years of age, he should know better than to have long hair. He always tied it back in a neat silver ponytail, never a hair out of place but they still called him 'that scruffy man.' Like his good friend, Mrs. Derbyshire, Arthur Ramsbottom was big-hearted seeing the funny side of everything. He had no time for the Greygoyles and their rules. Tiggy thought of him like a big teddy bear and just a very special person.

'Off somewhere nice?' he called to Tiggy, his left leg swinging out awkwardly as he walked over to see her.

Tiggy nodded and her dimples appeared for the first time that morning.

'Mrs.D's. Got a new move for the hols,' she said spinning the handlebars. 'It's called a 'Superman.'

Arthur loved hearing about her biking.

'More like Supergirl!' he said with a wink. 'You're welcome to try out my Bevvy's new bike if you like… she's not much call for one on a ship!'

'Thanks, but her old one's great! A BMX is perfect for the stuff I do. It's the tricks,' Tiggy replied.

'I bet Mrs.D will have a few tips and treats for you!' said Arthur offering her a polo mint from his pocket. Tiggy nodded.

The robin hopped onto Arthur's stick.

'It's so tame!' said Tiggy watching the bird peck the hooked handle.

Arthur smiled, staring at the robin.

'He's a very special visitor. I think he likes to check that I'm behaving myself.'

'A bit like The Greygoyles with me, then,' commented Tiggy with a bit of a shudder. 'They're at ours for The Residents Snots' Meeting.'

The two unlikely friends smirked at each other knowing that their feelings were the same about the people presently at Number 6.

'So, what do you think of your sunflowers?' asked Arthur changing the subject and pointing with his stick to a thicket of glorious golden blooms. 'Glad now you won them?'

He was looking up at the tallest that made him look small beside it.

'So weird a seed can grow so big!' said Tiggy sucking on her mint.

'Lots of TLC. Your TLC that's what did it!' responded Arthur, patting her on the head. 'No seed could want more than that my dear.'

Tiggy had absolutely no idea what TLC stood for. She had never heard of tender loving care, but decided TLC was the stingy stuff in a bluey green labelled bottle the teachers put on cuts and grazes at school. It was obviously powerful stuff.

'Shame father thinks they're horrible,' said Tiggy stroking one of the sunflower's ample leaves, her eyes burning into its rich coffee brown face. 'I worked my socks off in class to win that prize! Didn't look out of the window even once for three whole days!'

Arthur grinned.

'Still, they're yours. You like them and they like you. That's all that matters,' he said. 'I knew you'd turn those seeds into something special. I believe in you Tiggy Tipple,' he said patting her head. 'You have the magic power of being young. That means you can do just about anything if you really believe that you can.' He stroked one of the sunflowers petals. 'You've made my garden so beautiful!' he said proudly and she knew that he meant every word.

'Pity about this one though,' gestured Tiggy, squatting down to a sickly-looking specimen that was stunted and struggling to bloom.

'T.L.C. Tiggy....and a little patience,' reassured the man 'that's all it needs.'

Chapter 7

THE RESIDENTS WATCH MEETING

Back in the living room of Number 6, a lot of polite fakery had been going on but things were now turning nasty. 'Unacceptable behaviour' letters were to be leaflet dropped like confetti through the gleaming letter boxes of every home on the close. The newly arrived Riches were Item 3 on the agenda, not having got off to a very good start.

'Seven weeks they've been here and still no downstairs curtains!' moaned Mrs. Gibson.

'And they've four bratty looking children! Have you seen them?' Mrs. Grimshaw enquired. 'One of them had a football; it snapped off one of my roses!'

'So whatever did you do?' chorused Mr. and Mrs. Gibson.

'Smacked his backside of course!' replied Mrs. Grimshaw pretending to smack the gnome she was cradling.

'Little monsters waiting to grow into even bigger little monsters!' said Emily Gotobed.

'Little monsters waiting to grow into even bigger little monsters!' echoed Paul Gotobed.

'Children should be seen and not heard!' concluded Emily Gotobed looking as if she had a nasty smell under her nose.

'Children should be seen and not heard,' her husband repeated.

Frustratingly, the usually sensible and reliable Luvvies, were Item 4 having moved a foul-mouthed parrot into Number 9. Terence Tiddy, known locally as 'The ish Man,' was not happy.

'I heard it at twoish, three thirtyish, fourish and again at five fifteenish....a greenish, parrotyish sort of bird,' said Terence Tiddy thumping a magazine onto the coffee table as if he was fantasising about beating the bird.

'And it doesn't just squawk and talk. It swears as well!' added Ernest McAvey. 'You'd' think they'd know better!'

He was staring like a besotted teenager at Terence Tiddy whilst handing around his shortbread.

Alison Tipple looked at the magazine; a cover

model with blacked out teeth and drawn on moles and moustache stared back at her. Terence Tiddy had removed it from behind his cushion.

Suddenly, James Cartwright a wizened fellow, who as usual had sat quietly reading his bible, cleared his throat. Everybody knew it signalled that the old man was about to speak and yet nobody paid any attention. Then came his favourite one-liner of all,

'Is my coffin ready yet?' he croaked. Everybody pretended not to hear. Alison Tipple took full advantage of the interruption to offer around the Club biscuits and pink wafers whilst deftly removing the magazine from the table.

'Where's the vicar?' continued James Cartwright.

It was the first of many similar interruptions to follow, not that anybody could spare him the time of day. Life was too short and that was exactly his point. Everyone jittered uncomfortably. They were wondering whether anyone would be brave enough for a coded discussion about the funeral arrangements for Mr. Dodds, the thirteenth and latest C-U-R-S-E victim, but nobody dared.

The cravat-wearing Hugo F. Uppingham spoke how he dressed, and behaved as if he was in charge. He loved the sound of his own posh voice and had an answer and a rule for everything in the village. He was a pompous little man full of small-town ambition and described his fellow villagers as 'riff raff.' He persuaded the group to invite them to a meeting 'only as often as is necessary' to gain extra votes in next year's council election. The 'Residents and Villagers Association' was formed and a committee of 'R.A.V.As' duly elected.

'If we can bring ourselves to speak to these people, we can at least make sure that the Silver Jubilee celebrations will be tasteful,' Hugo F. Uppingham concluded. 'It may not mean having to let them into our homes but if we do, they don't have to use our china. Paper cups and any disposables will do!'

The room agreed with an enthusiastic chorus of 'aye ayes' but at the sight of Ernest McAvey brushing some shortbread crumbs off Terence Tiddy's knee and leaving his hand there far too long, a deathly hush fell over the room. It was awkward as if somebody had loudly passed wind and the agenda could not move on quickly enough to Item 7.

Timothy Grimshaw, an extremely dapper, blazer man, wearing an appalling wig reported the theft of one of their much-loved gnomes. For eleven years, Norman had fished from the Grimshaws' rock pool but had now been missing for 22 days.

'I've lost one of my babies! Please help us to find Norman!' Gertie Grimshaw sighed.

She was devastated, hugging the gnome she had brought with her and sobbing into its blanket.

However, there were clues. A series of postcards had turned up from Norman from various places around the Mediterranean. It set James Cartwright off again.

'How's my tombstone coming along?' he enquired. 'Do you think that this could be the last time I come here?'

'Coffin dodger!' mumbled Alicia Duncan Forbes, glaring at him through her icy eyes but her audience was still reeling from the news of a real-life crime on the close. It was very grave business indeed.

'Heaven forbid! It could be Mr. and Mrs. Potters' ornamental lions next,' chorused the Gibsons.

However, with everyone feeling jumpy about security, the Grimshaw's loss was to be Alison Tipple's gain. She proposed introducing a 'House-Sitters Roster' to the close.

'When people are away w...we make the h..h... home look occupied. R..r..removing p..post off the d...doormat, drawing c...curtains, parking a car in the dri-drive and that s..sort of th..thing,' she stammered looking at her feet, expecting a rejection.

The gnome theft made it a no brainer and the residents loved the idea. Alison Tipple felt quite overwhelmed and finally accepted as one of their own. She was now a regular on the coffee morning circuit and a few of them had started using her first name. Things were looking up.

It was just after mid-day when the meeting began to break up.

'What a fruitful gathering of astute minds!' Hugo F. Uppingham declared, sneaking the leftover shortbreads into his pocket.

The Gotobeds were the first to make a move for home, Mr. Gotobed carrying his significant other's handbag.

'What a wonderful meeting Mrs. Tipple. Shame Mr. and Mrs. Potter couldn't make it,' chirped Emily Gotobed like a budgerigar.

'What a wonderful meeting Mrs. Tipple. Shame Mr. And Mrs. Potter couldn't make it,' echoed Paul Gotobed.

'Thanks for the coffee, Mrs. Tipple....and I'll see you Tuesday...and don't do anything I wouldn't,' said Emily Gotobed, primly fastening her cardigan right up to its neck.

'Thanks for the coffee, Mrs. Tipple,' repeated Paul Gotobed and I'll see you Tuesday....and...'

'No you won't!' interrupted his wife, looking pleased with the opportunity to humiliate her husband in front of everybody. 'Not unless you've joined the Women's Institute without me knowing,' sniped Emily Gotobed. 'Honestly Mrs. Tipple....husbands!' she said rolling her eyes in sheer contempt.

Paul Gotobed checked himself, letting out a sigh

of relief, thankful that he had stopped himself from repeating his wife again, and left 'Pearly Gates' on her coat tail.

As soon as they had gone, they became the talking point, especially Emily Gotobed's legs. The bitching was ever so polite until Alicia Duncan Forbes, who had been sharing a quality moment admiring her own jewellery, joined in.

'Did you see the vile state of her legs? They have more varicose veins than a road map! And the hair! Ergh!'

Alicia Duncan Forbes shuddered and gestured in such a way that everyone would be sure to see her new diamond bracelet. It was no secret that the two women had never hit it off, both having far too much jewellery for the other to accept.

Further Greygoyles departed two by two, including Ernest McAvey and Terence Tiddy who resisting the urge to hold hands put them in their pockets. The remaining guests swapped recipes or newspaper cuttings, always sharing the gossip about those that had just left.

'I hope that pair won't start holding hands with each other!' snapped Alicia Duncan Forbes watching the two men walking up the road from the window.

'I wouldn't worry, they won't!' piped up Mrs. Gibson 'because they don't think any of us know.'

'Well at least that's something, I suppose. It would play havoc with our house prices!' the nasty woman concluded.

Nobody had brought up either the C-U-R-S-E or its thirteenth and latest victim, Mr. Dodds, apart from the brief mention of an opening for a new bell ringer if anyone should be interested. The first to arrive and the very last to leave, Alicia Duncan Forbes, by the time she had left, had more than lived up to 'The Bitch Queen' title that the remainder of the village had given her.

'Alison! I can see you and I are going to get along fabulously,' said Alicia peculiarly wiping her feet on the doormat on her way out.

Alison Tipple didn't care.

'She called me Alison!' she purred under her breath.

Chapter 8

THE STRANGER

The residents of Heavenly Gardens were experts at keeping up appearances. They did it all day, every day. Tiggy was rubbish at it even when she tried. The morning's full-out BMXing had left her looking a wreck and would trigger what the Tipple kids called 'The Sulk and Skulk.' Translated this meant their mother would be fuming and afterwards sulking and stammering, whilst 'Father' would lie low and skulk in his shed.

'Typical!' muttered Tiggy having already got as far home as the mill and wondering what to do about her filthy clothes. Suddenly the mill door creaked making her jump a little.

'Is that you Boggle? Have you got out of your barrel?' she asked peeping through the ivy.

Tiggy could hardly believe her eyes when a strange,

skinny boy emerged. She had no idea who he was or what he was doing there, and felt instantly annoyed seeing him in Mrs.D's mill, when she herself was the doorkeeper and had free reign of the place. She watched his every move for clues and as the boy headed towards the woods, she followed. He was frantically picking up sticks and had such a serious and purposeful manner he appeared to be there on a mission.

'Mrs.D needs to know about this!' she muttered as she sneaked commando-like from bush to bush, following him and trying to stifle the bonfire like crackle underfoot.

The boy had an unusual ghostly aura, moving without making a noise, like a scene from an old silent movie. His silence was golden and his presence serene.

'Ow you beast!' Tiggy yelped springing up from some nettles.

The boy immediately looked up, saw her, and ran, dropping his load as if it was a branding iron upon the skin.

'Don't go!' she shouted annoyed at having let out such a wimpy scream, but in a flash he was gone, lost to the shadows of the dark, tangled woods.

'I'm telling Mrs.D about you!' called Tiggy picking up the fallen sticks and discovering a pearl button shimmering amongst them.

It had to be his and slipping it into her top's pouch,

she now had the perfect proof for Mrs.D that he, a stranger, had been there.

Later when Tiggy returned to the mill to fetch her BMX the door was wide open. It had been empty the day before when she had disturbed the owl, but now the mill was full of wood and neatly bound sticks. The boy had to have been there and done all this. This was her safe place, dream factory, shelter and sanctuary. It had always been all of those things and now an unknown intruder had robbed her of her secret hangout. Several old flour sacks chocker with freshly cut logs stood by the door along with a woodchopper that glinted menacingly in the gloomy light. She thought about the C-U-R-S-E, scaring herself a little and when a huge rat scurried out of the shadows, she grabbed her bike to head for home.

Chapter 9

THE WOBNIAR

Tiggy would later describe the recent episodes in her diary as 'a load of mental goings on that I don't get!' The rat, intruder, strange puddle, the Mr. Dodds saga, the curse and the creepy singing from the tree had disturbed her. So many weird and inexplicable things had been happening that for the first time ever, Tiggy did not even feel safe at the mill. It had always been one of her favourite hideouts but now she felt panicked and disorientated, almost unaware of anything she was doing. It was a violation of her 'happy place,' as if the mill was no longer hers and grabbing her bike, a thousand thoughts bombed around in her head until she had a plan: she would tell Mrs.D about the intruder on her way home and get cleaned up to make herself more 'Heavenly Gardens friendly,' before returning to The

Close and setting tongues wagging. However, she was so preoccupied mulling it all over, Tiggy had ploughed straight into the mill's puddle, having forgotten that it was even there. This one small, split second decision was to have one epic consequence.

As soon as the wheel hit, the water sprayed up and her eyes' perfect vision melted into a dreamy haze. It was like one of those golden dreams that are so good you feel cheated if you wake from it too soon. You want it to keep going so that you can enjoy the wonderful world your head has created. Curiously, her handlebars were getting hotter and hotter too, forcing her hands to let go as the bars themselves began to rotate. She flat-lined, laying low along the bike's slanted crossbar, ducking clear of the bars that were now picking up so much speed they blurred like a helicopter's rotor blades spinning round. Tiggy could feel the firm grounding of her bike lighten beneath her body, as her trusted BMX, now weightless and unsteady, started to rise. The girl that had always bossed her bike had lost control, the 'ghost bike' directing her up and beyond. Tiggy clung on, sailing higher and higher in an exhilarating transit to another world.

The ghost bike carved its way silently through seas of mist, passing cloud after cloud floating like islands in a wonderful ocean. Each cloud was like a world wanting and waiting for her discovery. As unexpected and strange as it was, and even though her BMX felt so different, whether it was a ghost in bike form or not she did not feel scared. Tiggy loved the thought of owning her very own piece of cloud and was already planning to keep it in an old, empty Tate & Lyle treacle tin, (her favourite because of its lion trademark) that she had kept handy for a special discovery. Something as unusual as cloud she thought deserved it.

'ERGHH!' she sighed having grabbed at the cloud and watching it instantly disappear in between her fingers. 'What could be here one second and gone the next? How could something be nothing or nothing something?' she asked herself, making a mental note under 'something and nothing' for when she got home. Alex would know.

Just as dreams are able to make nonsense of time, place and in fact, pretty much everything, Tiggy's flight made little sense to her, too. Nothing seemed certain and without Alex who knew about most things, she had no points of reference. He would have known what was going on. Was she about to be the first girl in space, headed for a star or even the moon? He had told her about the Apollo moon landings, black holes in space and triangles in Bermuda that swallowed people up to disappear without trace, but not this. Tiggy soared past cloud upon cloud until she arrived at one that looked inviting to explore. It was like a jumbled stack of marshmallows and delicately outlined in silver. She clung on as the ghost bike disappeared into the milky softness.

Inside the raindrop cocoon, a pure white light enveloped Tiggy's body, like an invisible superhero defending her from the raindrops and keeping her dry. The light's brilliance was so overpoweringly harsh on her eyes that she did not see it refract, and when next they opened, seven bands of colour pulsated as if beating hearts. From each a different coloured mist gushed out spurting up in a volcanic display of power. It was a living, breathing rainbow. Suddenly, the spewing of mist subsided and out from the depths appeared a shadowy looking man seated upon a crystal throne. He was king-like with an obvious air of importance although there was a hint of Arthur Ramsbottom, but a sort of ghostly version. A host of softly singing angels surrounded the throne, a vision of serene beauty in their opal gowns, and rainbow wings that shimmered in the dreamy light. The angels were similar although different in small ways. That is except for one. In fact, it was so different that Tiggy was not sure that it even was an angel. There were neither wings nor halo and a downy, hairy tuft sprouted from its baldy head. Suddenly the angels stopped singing and Tiggy could have heard a pin drop. The man stared long and hard at Tiggy until eventually he spoke.

'Welcome Tiggy Tipple. We have been expecting you,' he said touching her lightly on the shoulder with a sabre flashing of rainbow coloured light. On his lap was a large golden book. It had so many pages it was like an ancient tome, the sort that makes a dull thud when it closes.

'I am The Wobniar, The Guardian of the Rainbow,' the man announced. 'You are here on your very own Rainbow Quest to journey through the sacred arc of colours, your Earth's emotional core where both good and bad energy is processed. You are a Rainbow Child with the magic of pure colour in your heart. Only children with this rare and precious gift can pass this richness to others. Your journey here and successful completion of your Rainbow Quest will enable you to restore colour to the darkest hearts and to cure the emotional root of all ills. May you now receive 'The Book of the Realms.'

The Wobniar touched the gilded book with his sabre.

'I bless this book's pages to reveal the Rainbow Quest in accordance with my Crystal Keeper's wishes,' he said.

An angel broke away from the choir and The Wobniar smiled and nodded his approval.

'May this Angel guide and keep you safe.'

The angel gathered up the tome and came to rest

by Tiggy's side. It was beautiful and radiated such a calm and gentle energy any anxiety was soothed in an instance. Tiggy felt confident that the angel was a 'she' and thought her gentle, sweet features and glowing halo of sunflowers made her the prettiest angel of them all.

'Angel Seraphina has been watching you closely and has chosen you to be her Rainbow Child,' said The Wobniar showing off his crystal tooth that out-glinted his bright eyes.

Angel Seraphina smiled and Tiggy could feel her force moving warmly through her body. It was a lovely feeling, like sunshine on skin. She stared at The Wobniar, this stranger, this being whose ethereal presence was unlike anyone or anything she had ever seen before. He had long, crinkled hair flashing like fibre optics through every colour of the rainbow and a magnificent cloak, made from a myriad of tiny mirrors, draped his solid frame. Tiggy stared at him, her mouth gaped open, mesmerised as her face flashed straight back like hundreds of 'selfies', from the garment's mirrors. A bird, with a bright red breast, just like the robin she so often saw in her garden, sat perched upon his shoulder and only when The Wobniar slashed the air with a series of strokes of his sabre and the hushed angels burst into choral song again did the bird fly away.

'Seraphina, Seraphina,

Guide, protector and friend,

A chaperone upon your shoulder,
Go seek the Rainbow's End.'

Angel Seraphina wrapped her rainbow wings, like a protective shield, around Tiggy's body, transferring to her The Book of The Realms. The connection between them felt strong and real and Tiggy's brain, that had been bombarding her with anxious questions, instantly felt at peace. They smiled at one another, Angel Seraphina's image gently fading away as Tiggy immediately sensed a lightening within her body. Her right shoulder was tingling, glowing with a celestial light and she felt a calmness and well-being she had never felt before. It seemed unearthly, even heavenly, and as the light absorbed into her body, Tiggy knew that her angel was with her. The Guardian of the Rainbow nodded his head in approval.

'It is time, Rainbow Child, to colour your destiny and to discover The Sacred Secret. This secret must not be shared with anyone or you will not return and will never reach The Rainbow's End. Angel Seraphina will lose her powers and you, dear child, will never receive your wings. Reveal the secret at your peril!' he said, his pale blue eyes piercing right through her with an icy intensity.

'She will wear the halo and not the horns,
Be the rose and not the thorns,
As your friend and not your foe,

Your angel is with you. Garashibo!'

The Wobniar flamboyantly waved his sabre and as it flashed through every colour of the rainbow, a breeze stirred amidst the serene gathering and 'The Book of the Realms' was flung open. The wind turned the pages in a frenzied flurry of flapping paper until eventually it settled, and Tiggy's Rainbow Quest revealed itself upon the page. A sea of multi coloured mist rose up, and Tiggy's legs wobbled a bit, her head spinning in a whirl of rapid movement, lost in time and space.

Chapter 10

THE RED REALM

When the mist had cleared, Tiggy was alone and her ghost bike had gone. The Wobniar on his throne and the angels were now like a dream and she was in a strange place, a bit like space in a fairytale. There was an abundance of rocks and dust whilst the spires of a dreamy fairy book castle enchanted in the distance. Whatever mysterious forces were at work she did not know, but here she was, confused and sat on a giant boulder holding The Book of The Realms. However, after the vibrancy and dazzling colours of the rainbow and her introduction to The Wobniar, perhaps the strangest thing of all was the now absence of colour. In fact, it was as if she had been dropped onto a black and white movie set but did not know what role she was to play. Her casting was, of course, to be the 'Rainbow Child' that The Wobniar had commanded.

Suddenly, a voice from behind the boulder startled her. It was a boy of teenage years and a strong American accent. He had the typical adolescent credentials of a bolted brace on his teeth and pimples.

'Careful with that, Miss!' said the boy pointing to 'The Book of The Realms.'

He held his hand out to her. Tiggy had never shaken hands with anyone before, nor had she ever met an American. This boy also had dreadlocks that she thought were most unusual in a cool and fabulous sort of way.

'Hi, I'm The Stig Man, or at least that's what my buddies call me at home in The States,' said the boy shaking his dreadlocks and grinning so that the bolts of his brace glinted at her.

The children shook hands staring at each other with the warm curiosity of strangers who hoped to connect.

'Tiggy, T-I-double G-Y,' she responded spelling out her name and noticing the dazzling blueness of the boys eyes sparkling beneath the matted rope-like chaos of his hair.

'I'm lost!' added Tiggy wondering if this strange American boy could help her.

'Better lost than trapped like me, Miss,' replied The Stig Man. 'I stupidly gave away The Sacred Secret when I knew not to, so now I'm stuck in the rainbow forever. I can help you though, Miss.'

They had only just met but Tiggy instantly liked him. His charming courtesy, cheeky smile and confident manner was so unlike the boys she knew. No boy had ever called her 'Miss' before. Besides which she thought his hair was the coolest she had ever seen.

'I've no idea what I'm doing here,' said Tiggy.

'Everything you need to know and do is in there, Miss,' instructed The Stig Man pointing to the hefty book. It contains the quest of every Rainbow Child, including yours. They're all different.'

Tiggy could not see Angel Seraphina but she could feel her presence warm and strong like a familiar comfort blanket melting her anxiety.

'Sure seems you need a bit of educating, Miss,' said the boy climbing up onto the rock to sit next to her. 'And I don't mean Math!'

'Good! I'm so rubbish at sums. Once I've run out of fingers I'm done for!' Tiggy jested looking closely at the boy's dreadlocks and longing to touch.

'This place is all about attitudes and feelings and how they're shaping you,' said the boy flicking his dreadlocks again. 'Call it emotional energy I guess, be it good or bad. The emotion from any single moment once expressed may appear to be gone and past but the energy from it remains. It isn't gone just 'cos a dude isn't feeling it no more,' he said looking closely at Tiggy to see if she understood. 'No, no, no! The energy is forever and has a life of its own so it has to end up somewhere, and that place is here.'

The two Rainbow Children were soon so comfortable in each other's company that they looked like they had always been 'Day One' friends. Tiggy knew that as a chosen Rainbow Child she had a lot to learn about this new world, her vocation and mission, but felt lucky to have The Stig Man who was so willing to share his wisdom. The Stig Man explained that the energy from our feelings and attitudes had its own coloured realm and arrived there for grading on a scale from pure to impure.

'It has to be colour matched, checked and stored, keeping the good energy away from the bad or it will all end up rotten like a black banana in a fresh fruit bowl. The Indigo is home to all the bad stuff. Not that I've ever been there.'

'I still don't get where I fit in,' said Tiggy wondering if there had been some kind of mistake.

'Every Rainbow Kid (and that's you Miss!) has a quest to win 'The Crystals of Change,' one crystal from each Realm and then you're ready for 'The Rainbows End,' said the boy taking a long pause and flicking his dreadlocks again.

'I love crystals!' said Tiggy.

'They're awesome Miss. They have special powers like healing, energising and all sorts that will change your destiny for the better. You are here for a reason, Miss. It's usually life changing.'

'But why me?' asked Tiggy secretly counting the boy's dreadlocks.

'Your Angel picked you. It had millions of kids to choose from but it picked you,' The Stig Man said shaking his hair like a wet dog. 'It knows it can help you.'

Tiggy's world, as she knew it felt upside down and unsafe, like being in free-fall unsure of a parachute. The trepidation was gnawing away at her gut until Tiggy sensed the velvet hand of Angel Seraphina reminding her she was still there.

'You sure need to open that, Miss,' The Stig Man said pointing to the 'Book of The Realms,' 'to discover your rainbow quest. No two Rainbow Kids have the same.'

Tiggy pulled back the book's cover and instantly everything became illuminated as if she had switched on a bright light. The landscape now dazzled with eye-catching accents and silhouettes in various shades of red unlike anything she had ever seen before.

'We're in The Red Realm,' declared The Stig Man. 'That means winning the red crystal by whatever quest The Crystal Keeper has decided.

'So have you completed your quest?' asked Tiggy gazing around at the landscape, amazed that one little action of opening a book had had such a dramatic effect.

'Nope! I foolishly gave away The Sacred Secret before I won all the Crystals of Change and my angel lost its power. Mine's the hairy one without the halo, Gregory Cecil, the punk angel!' said the boy. 'Without an angel to give their blessing there's no way into The Rainbows End, and no way home either.'

'So you're stuck here?' Tiggy asked already sensing that there was great pain in what he was saying.

'Sure am. I just miss going to the diner and playing baseball with my buddies. It sure feels ages since I scored a home run.'

He was fighting back the tears and trying to put on a brave face for his young companion's sake, who was only at the start of her journey and had so much to learn and do.

'I just wish I had respected that what happens in the rainbow stays in the rainbow.' The Stig Man blinked away a tear and composed himself, 'Miss Tiggy!' he said pointing to 'The Book of The Realms' and to a red light shining from between the pages. 'It's time to begin your quest.'

Chapter 11

THE WISHING STONE

A brilliant red light was shining from The Book of The Realms and knowing that there was work to do Tiggy turned the pages in search of the light.

'Don't worry about the blank pages. They belong to other Rainbow Kids and that's the reason you can't see them,' informed The Stig Man. 'Once they completed their quest and got to The Rainbows End their challenge became invisible for anyone else to see. They're still in the Book, just not there to us.'

Angel Seraphina appeared as a hologram through the dazzling light, her wings flittering and flirting with the page. Tiggy knew that this was the page that held the key to her quest. Angel Seraphina's holographic image faded and at that moment, the whole of The Red Realm stirred. Red admirals fluttered, ladybirds flashed past and robins flapped feathers in a spectacular whirl of colour. The Red Realm was finally awake. The Stig Man high fived her and kicked his feet through the sparkling dust. All around red rocks glistened and ruby-red roses perfumed the shimmering air with delicious scent. The Book of The Realms pulsated and an image slowly developed onto the page like an old-fashioned photograph in a dark room. It became a moving, living picture vibrating upon the page. All around a hazy red light throbbed. The Rainbow Children sat glued to the rock in a mystical suspense at what might be about to happen. They were like spies within a parallel dimension; not in a James Bond kind of way but similar to the first astronauts who when they went to the moon said that they had actually discovered the Earth. It was like a cosmic experience millions of miles from the world of Number 6 Pearly Gates, that had appeared on the Book's page before her eyes and that The Rainbow Children were now watching in a repetitive Groundhog Day sort of way.

Alison Tipple was reading Tiggy's school report and the image showed her to be no less angry this time than she had been before, once again rejecting the peace offering daisy and its giver, her youngest born child. A cloud of black dust stormed the rock. They could no longer see the landscape with its majestic castle but then a swirling tornado like vortex sucked up the black dust and blasted it out of the Realm to the forever darkness of The Indigo. The Stig Man spluttered as he choked a little on the dust.

'Bah! That bad energy sure is bitter. It tastes rank!' he said holding his throat.

The dust had cleared and The Book of The Realms pulsated again. An image of Penelope and Tiggy faded in on the page. The children watched as Penelope retrieved the discarded daisy and gave it to her sister with a loving embrace. A cloud of red dust swirled around The Realm, the air smelling sweet like candy as it sprinkled rosebuds in its path. Then just as quickly, the tightly closed petals of each bud began to open like velvet teardrops in a spectacular display.

'That's the power of love in action,' said The Stig Man clapping with excited anticipation of what was about to follow. Moments later all the roses were in full glorious bloom and one by one began gradually to turn into the most beautiful crystals that Tiggy had ever seen.

'Sure thought so!' said the boy flicking his dreadlocks and then doing it twice more as if in celebration of what they had just witnessed. 'That's cos it's the positive energy of unconditional love - love in its purest form - the really good stuff,' he said inspecting up close one of the newly formed crystal roses. 'It's now crystallised for all eternity. Only happens to the very best.'

The Stig Man put his hand to his eyes and stared into the distance at the castle.

'Karma Charmas!' he said pointing to a chain of bright red sparks that were snaking their way closer and closer towards them. 'They mustn't see me here with you, it breaks The Crystal Keeper's Code. The Crystal Keeper is their Governor and their job is to respect his Code just as we have to respect The Sacred Secret,' the boy said jumping down from the boulder.

The closer they got the more the bright red specks started to take shape until Tiggy could see a group of tiny red silhouetted beings dressed in crystal studded tunics who were collecting crystals on their way.

'Copy me!' the boy said spinning around and completing a series of swift hand movements with her. 'That's what I call 'The Special Buddy. I have a different one for my best chums and this one is ours. Remember it, Miss!' The Stig Man said grinning and spinning around to repeat the hand movements with her again. 'It sure was good to meet you, Miss Tiggy, but I'll see you next time. Good luck with your quest!'

He flicked his dreadlocks flamboyantly back and forth several times, and then The Stig Man was gone.

It wasn't long before The Karma Charmas had weaved their way as far as Tiggy's giant boulder but they were so busy collecting up the newly formed rose crystals that they failed to notice her. Angel Seraphina appeared to her again in The Book of The Realms and was now ready to reveal Tiggy's Red Realm Rainbow Quest. The book thudded shut.

The Rainbow Child clung on to Pirate Pants and as the warm tingling of Angel Seraphina's velvet hand caressed her shoulder, Tiggy knew that her angel's presence would guide her through the Red Realm to secure her special crystal. She gazed at the black and white surroundings, now shrouded in red mist and accents, and at the Karma Charmas whose silhouettes glowed brightly with positive energy. They were cute, big-hearted little creatures, their heart beating on their sleeve to the rhythm of their mood as they went about their business collecting up any new crystals within The Realm. They had picked up those from the roses and now were snaking back to the castle with their sparkling load. An inner voice told Tiggy to follow them, whether it was that of Angel Seraphina, her head could not be sure, but in her heart, she knew that it was.

Tiggy walked and walked yet the castle did not come any closer, remaining as elusive as if you reach up with your hand to touch the moon, but it was not long before she had arrived at a long, straight avenue of cherry trees. The glossy fruit dripped like blood-red drops from the drooping branches. A robin was hopping behind her as she weaved in and out of the trunks moving towards the castle. It puzzled Tiggy that the castle remained just as tantalisingly out of reach. Suddenly the robin swooped down onto a branch, chirped and picked a cherry off the tree, dropping it from its beak at her feet before flying away. Tiggy stroked the tree trunks and ran her fingers over the many words that they had etched into them, on some just a single word whilst others had several. It reminded her of Mrs. Derbyshire's lightning tree and its carvings. Tiggy shuddered, hoping that these would not be so scary, and as she walked from one tree to the next, reading the words aloud, their random arrangement began to take on a new meaning:

'There is a special power deep
within this cherry's stone,
Granted to a Rainbow Child
when the stone is thrown.
This stone holds the power to
make a single wish come true.
Be guided by your heart,
the Crystal Keeper challenges you.'

Angel Seraphina pressed upon her shoulder; the robin chirped. Tiggy knew what she had to do and picked up the fruit to eat. She ate away the flesh until she had stripped the stone bare. This was the wishing stone. The overripe fruit dripped and dribbled its crimson juice down her chin, splashing onto her white plimsoll below but she didn't notice because something quite remarkable had happened. The once elusive castle, so splendid with its pretty turrets, now towered high above her. Tiggy was amazed so suddenly to be there, and even more so when she heard a cry cutting through the hush. A pretty, tiny Karma Charma was slumped against the castle wall, weeping. Tiggy noticed that the heart on its sleeve was pounding erratically, sometimes quickly, sometimes slowly, as if it was mirroring the Karma Charma's dismay.

'My brother is a prisoner in the castle dungeon,' the creature sobbed. 'He's been stripped bare of his crystals to be banished to The Indigo. If that happens I will never see him again because a Karma Charma has never escaped from there.'

Her tears were falling to the ground and the outer glow around the Karma Charma's body had visibly dimmed. Tiggy looked at the feeble and fading heartbeat understanding that she must act quickly if the tiny Karma Charma was to survive. The cherry stone was glowing and warm in her hand. Angel Seraphina was guiding her every move.

Tiggy immediately cast the stone into the air and for a moment, it hovered as if frozen in time. She knew that this was the wishing stone and had the special power to grant a wish. Without hesitation or a thought for herself, Tiggy wished for the Karma Charma's safe return. Suddenly, there was a loud crashing of chains and the castle's drawbridge lowered as the gates mysteriously swung open. From out of the shadows, the Karma Charma's brother appeared running across the drawbridge and into his sister's open arms.

Nearby, a beautiful scarlet unicorn, with a shining red jewel at the tip of its crystal horn, was grazing and tossing its flowing mane. The Karma Charma's outer glows were bright again and their beating hearts skipping upon their sleeves. Tiggy knew that they were safe. The brother and sister embraced and at that moment a blinding red shaft of light beamed forth from the unicorn's horn, passing through The Rainbow Child's body and releasing the precious jewel.

Tiggy blinked repeatedly as if she had grit in her eye, unable to believe that she was once more with her bike by the Derbyshire's mill. Everything seemed the same as before except for the sparkling red jewel at her feet and a robin perched on the barrel, watching her. She looked up at the gloriously blue sky but there was no sign of the rainbow. The whole thing felt like a dream, but the crystal in her hand and the cherry juice stain on her shoes contradicted the voice in her head.

Chapter 12

FUN DAY EVE FEVER

The leftovers of a spotted dick and a table of dirty dishes were in the kitchen when Tiggy got home. This sort of lateness spelt trouble.

'Well?' said Alison Tipple, her raised eyebrows asking the question all by themselves.

Tiggy's eyes zoomed in on the bin searching for her lunch, fully expecting the dreaded special scary-glary look that mums do when her kid is 'in for it'. A fly was circling the bin loitering with intent like crows crowding in on road kill. Tiggy suspected that it had been feasting on her lunch.

'What a silly sausage! Flat out on the floor this morning in front of the neighbours!' said her mother frowning.

Tiggy gulped. So much had happened that she had completely forgotten about the earlier rather awkward incident but suddenly, her mother burst out laughing and did not stop. It seemed as weird to Tiggy as the Mona Lisa with a cheesy smile. In fact, her jaw dropped so low that the fly that had been scavenging the bin flew into her mouth and out again making her mother laugh even more. It was so out of character that Tiggy was not sure whether she should join in or ring for a doctor! The truth was that Alison Tipple was feeling triumphant. The morning's successful meeting had robbed the woman of her grimace that usually masked her otherwise pretty features, and Tiggy's food was still warm in the oven. Hearing the laughter, Alex and Penelope were there in a flash, desperate to see what could be going on.

The following day was the village Fun Day and was one of the most important on the Tipple's calendar, particularly so this year as Penelope was honoured to be Great Snubington's Fun Day Princess. Alex was taking it all very seriously and had insisted on a dress rehearsal using an old newspaper picture of Princess Anne on her wedding day waving to the crowds for guidance on the correct hand waving technique.

'Where's your crown, sis? A princess needs a crown!' asked Tiggy looking to see how her brother and sister were reacting to their mother who was hiccupping now instead of laughing.

'Mrs. Duncan Forbes is lending me the tiara she wore for her wedding,' responded Penelope, passing her mother a glass of water.

'Which one?' Alex quipped. 'She's a serwial bwide!'

'Ha ha!' jibed Penelope rolling her eyes. 'It's so valuable it was kept in a safe even before Norman went missing.'

Penelope twirled in her dress with excitement.

'I can't wait to hear the church bells ringing for the start of The Fun Day,' she said.

'That's not likely, Pen. Mr. Dodds has snuffed it!' Alex said staring at Penelope's fingers before correcting their wave position. 'They weckon the dweaded CURSE has stwuck again with yet another gwuesome death in the village! It's now a baker's dozen of victims. Isn't it horwific?'

Alison Tipple looked panicked at her son who was eager to share what he knew about the curse.

'Appawently, in 1928 twin bwothers were...'

Alison Tipple threw her glass of water at Alex to stop him from saying more.

'Stop talking about that! You know what they say about the curse,' she said before hiccupping again and handing him a towel.

The village Fun Day had been a work in progress for a long time in the Tipple household. Just a few big decisions remained. They were the ones that make the difference between success and failure, a mantelpiece of trophies or a mantelpiece with no trophies. Alison Tipple's painting of Mrs. Derbyshire's meadows was one such decision. It needed a frame and Alex, despite the soaking he had had from his mother, scanned the selection, his eyes purposefully ignoring the poker straight lines of poppies trooping the colour in red uniform blobs across the canvas.

'Love the clouds, Mum! That cumulonimbus is an absolute stwoke of genius,' he said pointing to what looked like a cauliflower in the sky.

Alison Tipple beamed at her darling boy as he scanned the selection of frames.

'Less is more!' announced Alex holding up a simple clip frame, not wanting his mother to humiliate herself by displaying such an artistic monstrosity in an ornate swept frame better suited to a masterpiece on a gallery wall.

'Perfection!' he declared peering over his glasses. However, his mother, who had The Close to impress, could not resist the very fancy gold alternative.

'Even better!' she said strutting off like a proud peacock with the gilded frame.

'Dwat and double dwat! I do believe Claude Monet,

the gweat poppy painter, has just turned in his gwave!' mumbled Alex under his breath.

Fun Day Eve fever was building outside too. A meticulous military styled operation was underway as Thomas Tipple, his shirt undone to his tummy button and his braces hanging down, was making his crucial Fun Day selections. He was a man with a plan and had been digging up his root vegetables, washing them with love in a bowl and weighing his very best. Thomas Tipple was fussing over his chosen carrots, radishes, parsnips and potatoes like an owner of a dog vying to claim 'The Best in Show' at Crufts. A robin had followed his every step, and when he moved to another spot, the robin did, too. It had a curiosity and liking for Thomas Tipple, and now perched on the handle of his spade. Thomas Tipple, so engrossed preparing his 'top contender' vegetables, had not even noticed.

The locals typically described Thomas Tipple as 'a bit of a funny old boy.' He was beanpole tall and looked very clever. His glasses were his biggest style statement; they were unstylish and dorky but Thomas Tipple didn't care. Right now, all that mattered was being able to pin point the tiniest kink, blemish or imperfection among his contender vegetables. He peered over the tops of his glasses that rested heavily upon his upturned nose making him look like he was in a constant state of disapproval whilst his face wore a frown as comfortably as feet in a pair of old slippers. He was an actuary by profession and loved talking about death and disaster, always making people aware of the statistics for its likelihood for anyone at any given time, whatever they were doing wherever they were in the world. He weighed up the risks to everything.

'Watch out for falling coconuts!' he would say every time somebody he knew was off to somewhere exotic. 'Death by falling coconuts is far more likely than by a shark attack but of course swimming in the ocean is not without its risks.'

Whether it was because the job made him that way, or whether it was because he was already that way so he did the job, it was difficult to say. It was a case of 'the chicken and the egg....' All doom and gloom, his favourite saying was that the only real certainty in life is death. Life and living was definitely a very serious matter indeed.

Thomas Tipple was measuring his rhubarb and runner beans, tweaking and improving their straightness with a bizarre homemade contraption, when his wife handed him a cup of tea. She was bursting to tell him about the frame she had chosen.

'Thank you, Sweet Pea! That's another job jobbed,' said Father, taking the Floral Fantasy teacup and going in for a kiss.

Tiggy, who was sneakily checking out the whereabouts of Sluggy and Huggy, saw it all and squirmed.

'That revolting behaviour hadn't better become a habit,' she muttered. 'They've freckles and moles old enough to remember Winston Churchill!'

Thomas Tipple was the king of sheds. He loved them. In fact, he loved them so much so, that he had three that were all completely different: The potting shed, The 'Just in Case' tool shed and 'The Jobs been jobbed' shed. In the first two, many garden 'jobs were jobbed' whilst the latter was a place to escape to and to relax after 'jobbing his jobs' for the day. He beckoned his wife into 'The Jobs been jobbed' shed. Super-duper and plush, it was fully carpeted with its own 'comfy chairs' and a filing cabinet jam packed with magazines. He had something on his mind and wanted to speak privately about it. Hattie Hipperson's recent gift of a bottle of sparkling wine to a judge had been the talk of the village, especially as the woman was a strong contender for Fun Day honours,

'She says it was a gesture of thanks for a small kindness,' said Thomas Tipple to his wife.

'And what sort of 'small kindness' are we talking about?' Alison Tipple enquired.

'Apparently, it was a rubber ring! Mrs. Hipperson claims to have been stung by a bee on her backside!' her husband replied.

Alex was sitting nearby, cross-legged like a Buddha,

drying off from his mother's soaking in the sun and reading about the Apollo moon landings.

'A wubber wing! That woman could sink The Titanic! She would definitely burst it!' Alex jested, grinning as he noticed the robin hopping towards him.

It was not in the least bit shy and pecked enthusiastically at his book.

'So Father, do you believe her?' continued Alison Tipple trying to hide her amusement at Alex's comments.

The vibe in the village was bitter and deeply sarcastic, the popular belief being that it was, 'a likely story!' The bitching, backstabbing and talk of bribes and stitch ups had been getting out of hand.

'Well, she can hardly prove it if her backside has been stung!' Thomas Tipple replied stroking a marrow as if it were a pet.

'Toadie calls her Fattie Hippobum!' interrupted Alex 'because his dad says she's a cheat and has got a big b...!'

'Bottom!' his mother corrected and finishing the sentence to avoid the 'bum' word.

Thomas Tipple scoffed at the thought of corruption and polished the vegetable even more vigorously with a handkerchief from his pocket.

'Probably because bribe or no bribe she has a better chance of winning than he does!' he concluded. 'By my calculations, 85% better!'

Most of the Greygoyles thought Hattie Hipperson was a liar and fair-minded Thomas Tipple really did not know who or what to believe.

'Still, just thinking about what happened to poor Mr. Dodds, should we really be worrying about it?' Thomas Tipple pondered. 'He certainly always grew a decent sprout! Who would have guessed that last year's Fun Day would have been his last? You just never can tell,' he said having settled upon his own best Brussels sprouts.

Tiggy had overheard the whole conversation but she could tell that despite his reflective comment about Mr. Dodds, that underneath it all, her father was rattled. She knew how much hard work had gone into his Fun Day exhibits but now he did not sound at all confident that he had done enough to win and was calculating his chances of winning, an exact percentage for every category. He seemed particularly concerned about his floral entries that she had already spotted in one of his sheds. Suddenly, a water bomb lobbed from the direction of the buddleia bush exploded upon her back.

'Alex! I know it's you!' Tiggy shouted sticking out her tongue and throwing her flip flops at the bush.

His snorting laughter was such a give-away. Thomas Tipple briefly stepped out from the 'Jobs been jobbed' shed to see what was going on.

'That's not great either,' he grumbled to his wife

removing the stray flip flops from the buddleia. 'We have a butterfly bush and no butterflies! It's most disappointing!' Thomas Tipple said eye-balling the culprit for the commotion still hiding behind the bush. 'I thought it would be packed with them by now.'

The 'Just in case tool shed' had a heavily bolted, double padlocked door. It was where her father kept the 'lucky' wooden Fun Day box and pail. The door was already open and smelt fragrant like an English country garden. On the shelves were boxed treatments and sprays for every garden pest 'just in case' one should strike, a mountain of fertiliser and compost bags filled a corner 'just in case' the garden centre ran out, every tool had its spare, 'just in case' one should break and even the spares had a spare and all 'just in case!' The 'lucky' Fun Day box with its special ventilation and lined out with polystyrene worms was there on the side already with a cucumber and runner beans that her father hoped were winners. Her Father used it every year.

'My vegetables have an overall 18% better chance of winning if I use this box,' her father had said at breakfast. He insisted it was scientific and not superstition.

Tiggy looked at the freshly cut cucumber nestled on top.

'Puny marrow!' she said scoffing at the stubby cucumber, having got her veg. mixed up. She swapped the cucumber for what she thought was more likely to win and soon a half grown marrow was in the box.

'A bit boring!' she said sneering at the healthy-looking selection of pencil straight runner beans that were all the same length, colour and blemish free. With so many curly and blotchy beans on the plants, there was still time to pick what Father called 'beans with personality' and win first prize.

The 'lucky Fun Day' pail was brimming with roses, lilies, carnations, dahlias and more besides. These were her father's very finest freshly cut flowers for exhibition but were still not yet fully open. Tiggy was not at all impressed. She thought about her wonderful sunflowers and Mr. Ramsbottom saying that it was that thing beginning with 'T' that had made them so spectacular. She remembered thinking that it was the stingy antiseptic stuff in a brown glass bottle. She would definitely find it if they had some because the shed was so highly organised.

'Stand in here long and it looks like you get tagged!' muttered Tiggy, noticing that everything seemed to have its own hook, shelf or drawer complete with laminated label. 'So many brooms!' she said to herself scanning an overwhelming selection along one wall. 'Too many!' she declared having spotted broken 'Wedding broom' and 'Not much good broom.'

There were many cupboards, too, and two were

almost out of reach. The first was locked and had a sign that read, 'Only to be opened in the event of war,' the second was white with a bold red cross and 'First Aid' painted on its door. A typed list of risk statistics hung from its handle that included 'bamboo cane fatalities,' 'contracting tetanus' and 'severance of toes by a spade.' Gardening, through the actuary's eyes, was a very dangerous pursuit and so his First Aid box was like a chemist shop. Tiggy looked inside and smiled, seeing a familiar brown bottle of TCP. The smell was strong and antiseptic but the flowers would drink it in like nectar from the Gods.

'That's another job jobbed!' she murmured having drowned the very last rose. She was convinced that she had given them an extra winning boost.

Chapter 13

THE MILL

Tiggy's bedroom was an Aladdin's cave of heart-felt treasures and memories. Her mother called it 'junk'. There were seashells from a family holiday, pine cones from their one and only forest picnic, a pot of feathers, sparkly bits, badges, scribbled smiley face notes from Alex (his version of the modern emoji), and a small Kodak instamatic camera. This stuff was on show on the chest of drawers and windowsill. However, hidden beneath the bed was a large biscuit tin storing her chewing gum monsters and toenail clippings, and she had named them all. Tiggy inspected her monsters. She had made one of nearly all of the Greygoyles and every day she would play with them as if they were characters in a soap opera.

'Just bring me my diamonds! I cannot breathe without my diamonds!' mimicked Tiggy with her chewing gum version of Alicia Duncan Forbes.

'Hard cheese they're in the Indigo!' said Tiggy crashing down the lid.

Tiggy picked up her recorder. Next summer, The Queen's Silver Jubilee was to be a huge celebration. She blew out The National Anthem note-perfect with her nose and then drew back the curtains. Her sunflowers, with their heads still drooped and crumpled were too tired to welcome the new day but the friendly robin was there pecking at the recently dug soil for worms. Tiggy's entry for the Fun Day art competition, a landscape inspired by her visits to the Derbyshire's mill, stood on her windowsill. Wilf, her first and only hand-moulded neon pink bubble gum monster, was guarding it. Her slightly dog-eared drawing on school paper was brilliant for someone so young and was miles better than her mother's version, and yet Tiggy was not happy with it.

'There's something important missing,' she said under her breath.

She flashed the sticks of delicate pastels across the sheet, dusting it with a spectrum of colour and quickly the picture was complete. The magic of the countryside now with its very own rainbow captured so beautifully upon a single sheet that it instantly beckoned you there,

Tiggy herself included.

As the front door clicked shut behind her and Tiggy cycled down the road, not a single net curtain twitched as Heavenly Gardens slept. The Grimshaws' newly acquired guard dog was proving to be hopeless in its job role and had not woken either. Only the whirring of the wheels broke the hush, the dew-laden air so pure that the daybreak seemed to breathe its new life upon her skin. At this early hour, it felt and smelt like a different world; sweeter, softer and fresh with hope.

Once out of the sleeping Close and through the gap in the hedge, Tiggy hummed as she pedalled, snatching off wild grass stems on her way. She passed the Lightning Tree at top speed, haunted by what she had seen and heard on her recent visit. Two magpies were perched back-to-back upon one of the boughs together, and yet somehow apart, and it amused her how in this regard they were so similar to the Gotobeds.

'Good morning Mr. and Mrs. Gotobed,' she saluted and hurtling up the track, left them for dust.

Soon the old mill loomed and surprisingly the puddle had grown drastically overnight despite it not having rained. Tiggy was worried for the Boggle in case he couldn't swim and decided to check out some armbands that she had spotted stashed away in the garage. The 'puddle' was not exactly a puddle anymore and was starting to look like something much bigger.

Tiggy looked up at the mill's broken sails, a forlorn giant stranded on an island. It was a puzzling change to a scene that had been unchanged for years. Rain had been sparse. In fact, there had been so little that even the old people had not said that it would 'do the garden good.' Nobody could remember the last time it had really rained and the ground had had a good soaking. Nevertheless, even a distance from the mill, waterlogged ground was making things tricky and if it were not for a pathway of logs that had mysteriously sprung up overnight, the mill would have been out of bounds. Tiggy still had killer rats buzzing on her brain from before but something wasn't right, it was all highly suspicious and could even be serious. If that was the case, Mrs.D needed to know and although feeling nervous, she gave the rickety doorframe a shove.

Coming out of the bright sunshine into the darkness, Tiggy couldn't see at first but when her eyes adjusted, she saw a boy standing in the musty shadows, up to his woolly ankles in water. He stared back at her like a frightened fox surrounded by a pack of baying hounds. It was the stranger who she had chased in the woods the previous day. He was scooping up the water with a bucket and pouring it into a metal drum, his dark eyes blinking rapidly as the harsh light filtered inside.

'Hi, I'm Tiggy Tipple...double g, double p', she said with a huge grin, picking up an empty tin to join in and as she took her first scoops of water the sun's eye streamed through the door cracks, semi-illuminating her head to angelic effect. It was as if Tiggy was wearing a halo.

'Gawd knows where it's coming from,' Tiggy said looking as confused as a Victorian farmer in a busy tube station. 'My brother would know. He's a boff!' she said looking for a reaction. 'He does this weird maths thing in our garden with a forked stick that searches for water….a water divider I think he calls it. Alex says that we're going to find our own underground spring one day…then we will bottle it and become millionaires. Jokes!' she said whilst rolling her eyes, 'Water! Who would buy it?'

The boy ignored her and continued to work, head down, as if she was invisible.

'Did you know this village has a curse? Not many have one of those,' she boasted, but the boy showed not even a flicker of a reaction, nor interest. 'Mrs. Derbyshire says that I'm to treat the place like it's my own. Mrs.D is a top lady and teaches me loads of useful stuff.' Tiggy racked her brain for something to gain his attention. 'Did you know if you leave the hairy end bit on an onion when you peel it, it won't make you cry, and when a feather appears, angels are near, or if a robin pays you a visit it's bringing you a message from a loved-one you're missing? Mr.D's robin comes to visit us!' said Tiggy, her dimples dancing on her cheeks and the cat like brilliance of her eyes melting away the boy's shyness so that he looked up at her.

'Anyway, why do you want all these logs? It was me yesterday in the wood,' she asked.

There was a heavy pause and the boy coughed nervously.

'It's for my father,' he whispered hoarsely, shrinking inside his clothes as if he expected a slap, 'Its firewood.'

Tiggy thought how different he was to the boys at school, who were mostly lazy and annoying, trying to scare the girls with 'killer slugs' in the loos or burping 'deadly germs' over the library books. This boy wore a mask of serenity: he seemed remote despite being so near. In fact, he was like a shadow.

'It's so we're ready for winter,' the boy added. 'My father says that if you 'fail to plan, you plan to fail.'

'Sounds like mine! The grey hair and big pants are what does it and 'cos there's always a job needing to be jobbed,' said Tiggy noticing for the first time that the boy had lots of scars, and wondering what the story was.

He didn't look like he'd ever had much fun, and her mind began to spark like a giant firework, ideas fizzing and exploding in her head until she could contain it no longer, and with her eyes shining and craving adventure, she beckoned the boy out of the mill. He was nervous. Tiggy needed some action and in her opinion, he needed some fun. She would show him just what a girl could do on a bike and standing up on the BMX's pedals with the anxious boy clinging on tightly behind, she speeded off towards the woods. The more uneven the track the faster she went, zooming past the abandoned tractor, and heading straight for a mound of manure. The stench in the heat punched hard on the nose but at the last split second, just when it had seemed too late to miss, the bike's brakes screeched, skidding abruptly to a halt, centimetres from the steaming, stinky manure. Tiggy was on fire loving the thrill, the danger and having a passenger to impress and as she headed back towards the windmill she hungered for more.

'Hope you can swim!' Tiggy shouted seeing the mill with all its water coming into shot.

Her mind was set. The allure of the water was like a magnet to her and they hit it at top speed. The impact was spectacular, her thirst for drama quenched in an instant. Water gushed up from the wheels, the spray drenching the drought-dried dirt track and filling the cracks. The handlebars were hot and spinning fast like blades again. Her ghost bike was back and her companion inexplicably and without warning, had gone. Moments later, in a way similar to a moth attracted to a light, Tiggy's ghost bike was pulled by an invisible force too powerful to resist.

Chapter 14

THE ORANGE REALM

Tiggy had entered The Orange Realm of the rainbow. The Book of The Realms was already lying open as if it had been waiting for her. It was a pity that The Stig Man wasn't doing the same. She knew what Alex would have to say about the situation.

'Boys let girls down...Fact!'

Tiggy hoped for once that her wise and sensible brother would be wrong. This realm, too, was like a black and white movie set, but this time with striking amber accents of marmalade-coloured rocks randomly scattered upon a blanket of rainbow dust. Tiggy's footprints left a trail but there was no sign of anybody else ever having been there. It was just her and Pirate Pants, desolate and alone with The Book of The Realms pulsating and glowing bright.

'BOOM!' a voice came from behind so loud that it made her jump. It was The Stig Man.

'Thought you had quit your quest, Miss Tiggy, 'til I saw your footprints in the dust.'

Tiggy was so happy that her brother had been proved wrong and the trapped Rainbow Child had kept his promise. She tugged at the sock tying up the boy's dreadlocks in a playful kind of greeting.

'Excuse the briefs!' said The Stig Man. He was wearing his underpants superhero style over the top of his trousers. 'It's how I know what day of the week it is. Briefs inside out, back to front, outside my pants or even a combo. I've one for every day of the week,' he boasted.

That's genius!' responded Tiggy as they did 'The Special Buddy'. They both laughed not really knowing why but they did. The Book of The Realms was flashing orange and moving pictures filled the illuminated page again.

'That's my friend Mr. Ramsbottom. I call him my dream keeper,' informed Tiggy, her eyes glued to the page as her neighbour's image appeared.

Arthur Ramsbottom was in his garden staring and smiling at the sunflowers Tiggy had grown. Suddenly, a cloud of positive energy gusted into the realm almost knocking the children off their feet, lashing their hair in every direction as grubs began raining down like orange drops, one of which landed at Tiggy's feet. It was a huge, hairy, orange caterpillar. Tiggy knew that, as a Rainbow Child, she had the privilege to witness what others would never have the chance to see and she hoped that something spectacular was about to happen. The grub writhed and stretched, and stretched and writhed, and then with a wiggle and a jerk, the caterpillar exchanged its ribbed hairy vest for a smooth, dull, silky cased cocoon.

Arthur Ramsbottom's image still glowed from the 'Book of the Realms' and this time Tiggy was with him. He was giving her his granddaughter's old BMX. Another gust of positive energy followed and this time the cocoon burst open and from the silky casing emerged the most beautiful orange butterfly that Tiggy had ever seen. More cocoons with smaller butterflies were hatching one by one and in their hundreds, all of them orange and perfect. The children looked on in wonder as the insects twitched open their wings, flew around them a few times before crystallising. During this time the largest and most spectacular butterfly and the first to hatch, fluttered around the realm until coming briefly to nestle upon her shoulder. Tiggy felt the warmth of Angel Seraphina surge through her body and then as if it, too, had received the angel's blessing, the butterfly flew away into the distance and out of sight.

'Woah! Free butterfly status for that one. It had so much positive energy that it can even leave the Realm. It will end up in somebody's garden for sure,' said The Stig Man looking very thoughtful. 'Sure is a bit ironic when I'm stuck here, don't you think!'

Tiggy gave his hand a comforting squeeze. There were orange crystals everywhere, all newly formed by the gusts of positive energy from the image in The Book of the Realms. A hoard of tiny figures scuttled past the children swarming like bees around honey to collect them. Tiggy stared at the orange outer glow hugging their bodies and the fluorescent bubble yo-yoing from their tunic sleeves by an invisible thread.

'Orange Karma Charmas and they're their desirabubbles,' explained The Stig Man, 'full of the Realm's good stuff like confidence, enthusiasm, determination, encouragement and optimism. Only 'The Dreamstealers' have the power to pop them,' he said. 'They have enough power inside to feed the dreams and desires of every Rainbow Kid from here to Timbuktu.

'Who is Tim Buktu?' Tiggy asked never having heard of the place.

'Gee, you're funny, Miss Tiggy! Man I sure dig the Brits sense of humour.'

The Stig Man was unaware she hadn't been joking.

The Book of the Realms started to flash again. It had

more to offer and soon an image emerged of a defeated Thomas Tipple digging up his lupins and giving them to Tiggy to burn. The negative energy in the form of black dust stormed the Realm, the putrid smell like something rotting. Tiggy gagged, a little embarrassed in front of The Stig Man who seemed unaffected by the stench.

'I sure have gotten used to some rank stuff here. Seeing you like that, Miss Tiggy, has made me realise how long I must have been here. That used to happen to me.'

The dust was swirling like a storm of badness stinking out the place. Tiggy gagged again.

'Man! So much negative energy!' he said watching as the blackness disappeared. 'It sure will soon be in The Indigo.'

'And good riddance to it!' spluttered Tiggy recovering from her gag reflex position.

The children laughed at the same time to all the same things. It seemed like a friendship written in the stars.

'So what was that about? That picture of the man burning flowers?' asked The Stig Man.

'That was my father,' replied Tiggy.

'Why the fire?' enquired The Stig Man, removing the sock from his dreadlocks so he could flick them out. He wanted to look cool and impress her.

'He had to get rid after the bug attack. He says he's quit growing lupins!'

The Stig Man's eyes lit up like a light bulb moment of realisation.

'I get it! So this place is all about not giving up and self-belief. That's your journey right here,' he concluded.

'Oh, right! Mr. Ramsbottom is my dream keeper and he says I should believe in myself and it's good I'm ambitious. He reckons I can be a biking champ if I put the work in,' Tiggy said, taking Pirate Pants from her rucksack and adjusting the bear's eye patch to cover its missing eye. 'Isn't that right Pants?' she said, convinced that the panda understood. 'So, is that why the grubs turned to butterflies and the butterflies turned to crystals?'

'Exactly Miss Tiggy!' said The Stig Man looking pleased that his student was showing so much rainbow wisdom. 'My orange mission empowered me to think that ANYTHING was possible: climbing Everest, running the New York marathon, even bowling my buddy, Ashwin, out at cricket. I've never even played the game 'cos I'm more of a baseball 'Home Run Getter' kinda guy.'

'I really, really, really love cricket though I shouldn't; at home they say cricket's for boys, and rounders for girls. Stupid if you ask me! I can hit and catch as good as any boy.'

'I just wish I had respected 'The Sacred Secret. I was doing so well with my Quest until Gregory Cecil, my angel if you can call him that, sprouted hair and lost his power. I guess it's like Samson but in reverse.'

The Stig Man's sunny disposition was suddenly under heavy cloud. He was homesick.

'Life sure is just a matter of colour. We choose it every day. Grey and 'glumpy' as I call it, for one dude, may be orange and hopeful for another. One dude's problem is often another dude's opportunity,' he said his mood brightening.' A beginning to one may be an ending to another, and a 'problem' to me may be an 'opportunity' to you. Attitude, Miss Tiggy, is the simple difference. What happens to the energy in this place proves it. In my opinion, Miss Tiggy, energy is king. You have either positive or negative and it makes you or breaks you.'

'That's smart!' said Tiggy nodding Pirate Pants' head in agreement for him.

The Book of The Realms flashed several times again with a blinding orange light and Angel Seraphina's hologram appeared on the page.

'It's Sacred Secret time, Miss Tiggy. I must go. See you soon.'

The Stig Man tied his sock around his dreadlocks into a ponytail again before they did 'The Special Buddy,' and then he was gone.

Tiggy concentrated on The Book of The Realms and her Angel's love shone through her entire body. This was what Alex would describe as 'cwunch time.' The Rainbow Child would not remember what happened next but a silvery voice whispered to her somewhere deep down inside,

'A dream is a journey your heart yearns to take,
A crossroads for happiness
and decisions you must make.
Those who fear the failure
Bear forever scars,
But those who reach for the moon
Can but fall amongst the stars.
Beware of all who seek to steal
The stuff your heart believes,
For those who steal a dream
are the kings of thieves.
So reach out, reach out some more,
Chase, persevere, pursue.
Be true to yourself my child,
And to the dream that makes you, you.'

The Book of The Realms closed with a thud. Everywhere around her slept, and all was quiet and deserted except for an eerily beautiful tree that drew The Rainbow Child towards it. A unicorn with a beautiful, flowing mane dusted with sparkling citrine was asleep at the base of its gnarled and generous trunk. Tiggy thought it was the most magical creature that she had ever seen. There was neither a breath of movement nor a sound, just clouds of sparkly dust which puffed up with her every footstep, leaving a trail behind.

Suddenly a high-pitched chirruping from the tree cut through the hush. It was coming from a hollow set deep into its trunk and from a nest inside. Tiggy could see that it had once been full of eggs but now only one remained. Amongst the chalky fragments of shell, three newly hatched fledglings were discovering their wings and preparing to fly. Tiggy watched waiting to see which bird would be brave enough to leave the nest. Which would have the confidence, the self-belief and determination to succeed?

The nervous fledglings saw her and as if she had pulled the trigger of a silent starting pistol, two of the baby birds took the leap of faith and flew. The third remained teetering on the edge, looking out to freedom. It flapped its wings but then retreated into the nest again. Tiggy watched and waited, willing the bird on its way, but time after time, when the fledgling stood at the brink only its self-belief took flight. Tiggy thought about her Head Teacher's favourite saying, 'He who says he can and he who says he can't are both usually right.' It was on every classroom wall.

'Believe!' she whispered stroking the fledgling's warm feathers and cradling it in her hands.

The word echoed and echoed until the tiny bird forced open her hands and without further hesitation, it flapped its wings to go. This time with a sudden surge of confidence, the bird took off.

'Look Pants!' she said removing him from her kangaroo top's pouch to see.

The bird was changing in flight before her eyes. It was becoming bigger and more powerful by the second, until the transformation was complete.

'WOW Pants! It's an eagle!' Tiggy exclaimed, astounded by what had happened.

She watched the bird in awe soar further and further away until it was a distant orange speck.

Tiggy had done what she needed to do. The leaves on the tree began to crystallise as the unicorn with the citrine mane woke up. It tossed its mane and beamed an orange shaft of light from its crystal horn onto the one remaining egg in the nest. The egg lit up with a fire-like haze and the shell instantly cracked open, spilling out a beautiful gleaming crystal.

Tiggy found herself back with her bike by the mill admiring the reward she was clutching in her hand. This was her second crystal to keep safe and with the village Fun Day on her mind, she headed for home with the scrambled thoughts of rainbows, runner beans and roses.

Chapter 15

THE FUN DAY

The same empty milk bottles were still standing on the same doorsteps. Tiggy had beaten the milkman and was home before breakfast. She was dying to see what had happened to the Fun Day flowers overnight but as soon as she set foot on the lawn, the smell of antiseptic coming from 'The Just in case tool shed' killed all hopes she had of a miracle.

'Ahhhhhhh!' Tiggy screamed discovering that all the flower heads were drooped like mourners at a funeral. Alex heard her through his open bedroom window.

'Father will kill me if he finds out!' she wailed to Alex who had magically appeared at the first signs of drama.

He loved it. Her brother drew his index finger across his throat as if enacting a gruesome killing and then grinned.

'Father left extwa early for work. You'll live!' he said examining a sickly looking rose.

'I thought it was his day off!'

Tiggy was surprised that he had gone to his office when it was not only a Sunday but the Fun Day too.

'It is!' Alex responded. 'He's got some jobs needing to be jobbed first. You know what Father's like. That's why he's got his own key to the office!'

An orange butterfly circled the children, hovered for a bit and then flew into the nearby flowerbed. This was a Tipple crisis of epic proportions and there was nobody better dealing with these situations than Alex.

'I do love a family dwama. Fetch me some cutters sis'!' Alex ordered. Moments later the unlikely superhero, still in his paisley pyjamas, was storming the flowerbeds to save his little sister's skin.

'Off with her head!' he yelled with every severed stem until but a few flowers were left standing. Alex puffed out his chest.

'Weminds me of the Fwench Wevolution.... decapitated heads everwywhere,' he said admiring his work.

The orange butterfly had returned and landed firstly on Alex's shoulder and then fluttered onto Tiggy's hand to settle.

'Well, the signs are pwomising,' Alex said staring at the butterfly and smelling the flowers he had just cut.

'Butterflies symbolise change about to happen in your life, and when it's owange like this exotic cweature, it means something joyful and bwilliant is going to happen. I weckon we have this nailed!'.

The butterfly stayed a while and Tiggy recalled the magnificent butterfly that she had watched achieve 'Free Status' in the Orange Realm. Her eyes were glued to it until eventually it fluttered away.

'Bye, bye Orange Realm butterfly!' she called. 'Is it you?'

The Fun Day took place on the village 'Rec.', the recreation ground by the village church. Once a year all of Great Snubington got on together. However, only a stranger to the truth would have believed it. In reality, the village was divided between the old and new, enemy lines falling roughly by the Village Green. The old villagers, who thought they were the 'proper villagers,' had lived there for at least three generations. Put simply, if you could remember the opening of the village post office and Mr. Porter's dog delivering the morning papers, you were one of them. The 'newbies' had moved in when seventeen years prior, two new housing estates had sprung up, the smallest of these being Heavenly Gardens and its peacock-proud residents. The newcomers would remain so until the last surviving person of the 'proper villagers' who could remember them moving in had died. It was that sort of community, and the only thing that really united them was their universal respect and concern for the curse.

At midday, the 16th Great Snubington Fun Day got underway without the usual peal of bells and of course, no Mr. Dodds. However, despite being a village in shock that the curse had struck again, everyone was doing their bit to carry on. An open-horse drawn carriage arrived with the village's Fun Day V.I.P.s, Lord and Lady Butcher, sitting opposite pretty Penelope Tipple, Great Snubington's Princess for the day. Penelope's smile lit up the place, the princess waving exactly as rehearsed at home. Tiggy clicked a couple of shots with her instamatic camera hoping she had captured a good expression but it was so hit and miss that it was impossible to tell. Penelope spotted her family in the crowd and gave a little wave but disappointingly 'Father' was not there, he was still 'jobbing a job' at his office. She forced back her tears and manufactured a smile as she cut through the ribbon and unveiled a new bench in fond memory of 'Knit More Nora' who had recently passed away at the village's record age of 102 with her knitting needles still in her hands. It had been nothing to do with the curse. As soon as the crowds began to scatter, Alison Tipple moved in on her eldest daughter, hairbrush poised.

'Nice one, Sis! Pwincess Anne couldn't have done it better,' remarked Alex patting his sister on the back, aware that their mother did not look at all happy.

'They'll say we're getting too big for our boots!' said Alison Tipple yanking at her daughter's hair with the brush. 'You know Lord Butcher always cuts the ribbon. Whatever were you thinking?'

Penelope's smile went out and Tiggy's eye roll said it all. The sight of Alicia Duncan Forbes laden down with jewellery heading towards them to check on her tiara was enough to make Tiggy run for cover.

The stalls boasted guess the weight, name, spot or number of just about everything under the sun. By the bouncy castle, the stocks were attracting big crowds and the first victim was the village vicar. Mikey Mucus, whose middle name should have been 'obnoxious,' had barged his way to the front of the queue to hurl the gunk. He was a sporty lad who played in the village cricket team. He never walked the length of a room or down the road without pretending to bowl a ball every few yards. It was therefore, no surprise when his fierce, fast arm hurled down a handful of the sloppy peas' slime scoring a direct hit. Eventually the vicar pleaded for his release.

'Peas, peas…I mean please,' he said theatrically, 'no more peas…I need to spend a penny!'

'He means he needs a pee!' shouted Mikey, hurling

another handful of the ghastly pea concoction at the trapped and helpless Vicar.

The crowd roared; Mikey laughed, showing off a mouth boasting more fillings than a sandwich factory, and wiping his ever-familiar runny nose with his sleeve. A small child noticing the boy's black teeth began to point and sneer.

'Okay squirt! I like sweets! Big deal!' snarled Mikey and he walked off gesturing rudely before fake bowling again.

Great Snubington's Marching Band and Baton Twirlers were in the arena strutting and banging drums. Batons were tossed, a few even caught and when a little girl stopped drumming to hitch up her knickers, the crowd loved it even more.

Nearby, in the beer tent, Ernest McAvey and Terence Tiddy sat together trying to hold hands beneath the trestle table. They were hopelessly in love but nobody was meant to know, or at least, not officially, but it was obvious by how they could not help gazing into each other's eyes. The local ale was flowing and Morris dancers were downing pints before they had even jingled their first jig. The Greygoyles were out in force, moving in packs, each wearing a black armband as a mark of respect to Mr. Dodds. Tiggy felt much safer from their disapproval disguised by her new tiger face paint. It was worth every penny not to be recognised.

Mrs. Grimshaw was taking a turn at running the 'Guess the Weight of the Pig' stall, but as much as Tiggy wanted to see 'Churchill,' who was on loan from Mrs. Derbyshire, she decided to give it a miss. Ever since Norman the gnome had been missing, Gertie Grimshaw viewed everybody with suspicion and Tiggy in particular found her fixed starey glare following her wherever she went.

Tiggy bumped into Arthur Ramsbottom by the tombola stall. He recognised her instantly beneath her disguise.

'Well, if it isn't my favourite 'Tiger Tig!' I've been looking for someone to treat!' he said fumbling in his pockets. 'I bet you'd like an ice cream!' and slipping her a handful of coins he pointed to the 'Mister Softee' van.

Tiggy loved ice cream, but as one of her mother's 'seven edible sins' she was hardly ever allowed one. An untidy queue had formed at the van, entire families often standing together pushing out the line and obscuring the view of the serving window and the picture display of ice creams on the side of the van. Even standing on tiptoes, a giant haystack of a man kept blocking Tiggy's view. Fed up with waiting he suddenly moved away and standing there right by the serving hatch was no other than the boy from the woods. Tiggy moved and jostled, giving the queue a bit of sharp elbow action to get a better view, but as soon as she had worked her way far enough to see properly, he had gone.

'I know you're here somewhere!' Tiggy muttered having bought her ice cream and scanning the crowds.

Mikey Mucus with his fast arm was celebrating first place in the Welly Hurling, his khaki boot having beaten the vicar's old-fashioned black by three boot lengths. A huge eagle was watching everything from its display stand. Tiggy stared at the bird and it stared directly back, its feathers looking like glistening amber in the light. Now that the eagle had spotted the girl, its piercing eyes followed her. As strange as it was, it was as if there was some kind of connection. Tiggy took a few steps closer to the stand, her mind racing back to her last rainbow adventure in the Orange Realm.

'Er, are you the baby bird I helped to fly?' whispered Tiggy.

Suddenly, the throb and revving of engines drowned out the nearby music as a team of a dozen motorbikes entered the arena on their back wheels and wheelied into the arena. For Tiggy this was the highlight of the Fun Day.

'I've been waiting all year to see this!' she said, having returned to Arthur Ramsbottom as pairs of riders sailed through the air, crossing paths at the mid-point and narrowly missing each other by a whisker.

'Woah! That was close!' squealed Tiggy each time the riders landed safely on the other side.

The ice cream had been melting more quickly than she was eating it and was dripping everywhere. Arthur Ramsbottom handed her a neatly folded handkerchief from his pocket.

'They were amazing!' Tiggy said wiping her hands on it and looking for Arthur Ramsbottom's reaction.

He looked different. A pinkish haze was hugging the outline of his body. Arthur Ramsbottom seemed unaware of it but she hoped that perhaps her mother, who was walking towards them, would see the glow and say something. However, Alison Tipple was too busy giving his ponytail the glare and noticing some ice cream on Tiggy's collar, she lunged towards her daughter with a freshly spat-upon tissue. At that moment, the gorgeous Madeleine Beau Ellison glided by in a low-cut but tastefully tailored dress. Her sunglasses were perched on the top of her head and a large floppy bow secured her long, voluminous, chestnut brown hair. The village beauty had an air of unaffected chic, catching the eye of everyone. A Mexican wave of turning heads rippled through the crowd as males and females alike stared at the vision of loveliness.

'I'm surprised she doesn't dislocate her hips with that walk of hers,' scoffed Alison Tipple as Madeleine Beau Ellison elegantly slunk by.

Arthur Ramsbottom chose not to hear.

'As for this lot,' she hissed glancing across to the

riders and their wheel tracks on the grass, 'they've ruined our field....the R.A.V.A.'s will be raving mad!'

She flounced off, secretly in awe of Madeleine Beau Ellison, attempting to slink her hips as best as she could in the direction of a group of Greygoyles gathered outside the First Aid Tent. A giant straw hoop had been set alight for the motorbikes big finale. The flames leapt, the engines throbbed and the fume-filled atmosphere was electric. Everyone anticipated something special. The leading rider zipped away towards the ring of fire and took off into the flames. Each cyclist followed, launching into the blaze and emerging safely on the other side to huge cheers from the crowd.

'Now that's what you call 'playing with fire!' joked Arthur Ramsbottom.

'They were ace!' Tiggy shouted over the noise of the engines as the cyclists waved their way out of the arena to great applause. 'It's my dream to do something like that. Why should it just be for boys?'

'No reason!' said Arthur Ramsbottom. 'You just have to change the way people think.'

'He's the British champion,' informed Tiggy pointing and waving at one of the helmets. 'But Father always says, 'what's the odds? Only one in a million will ever be a champ so there's no point even trying.'

Tiggy searched her friend's eyes for a contradiction.

'Alex got a goldfish bowl stuck on his head and had

to go to hospital. He never dared to admit that it was because he wants to be an astronaut. The odds are bad. That's why he's always singing Dave Bowie songs about space.'

'Um,' Arthur Ramsbottom carefully pondered his response, 'it has to come true for someone. There's nothing wrong with having a dream, Tiger, in fact, I reckon that everyone needs one.'

Tiggy couldn't take her eyes off him. The strange glow surrounding him was getting brighter.

'Even an oldie like me likes to dream sometimes,' he continued, 'I often dream that I'm......'

A kerfuffle near the First Aid tent brought him up short. Gertie Grimshaw had had a funny turn but nobody was laughing.

'It will be Norman,' said Tiggy, 'he's gone missing and has been sending postcards from loads of places abroad, Monte Carlo, Navels.'

'Naples!' corrected the old man, smiling.

'Alex says its ice-cream heaven so no wonder Norman's gone there.'

Arthur Ramsbottom had a mischievous glint in his eye.

'What a coincidence! My Beverly's ship has just sailed from Naples!'

The talk was that Gertie Grimshaw had been feeling unwell ever since a postcard had mysteriously appeared on the Fun Day event's board demanding a ransom for Norman's safe release.

'Five packets of sweeties by midnight tomorrow,' snivelled Gertie Grimshaw.

'Or else the gnome gets it!' said Timothy Grimshaw reading from the card.

'Preposterous!' said Emily Gotobed.

Tiggy looked at the woman's legs. Everybody did. 'Preposterous!' echoed her husband.

'Everyone knows that Norman's worth far more than a few bags of sweets,' sobbed Gertie Grimshaw. 'We have honestly never been so insulted,' she continued, weeping into her lace handkerchief.

'Sounds like a gnomenapping,' remarked Arthur Ramsbottom to his little companion. 'I've a feeling that Norman will turn up again soon, sweets or no sweets,' and he winked putting his fingers to his lips as if he had just confided in her the world's biggest secret.

The star act of the day was a somersaulting six-pack of a man called 'The Mad Maxeman.' He tumbled into the arena in silky blue breeches and a matching waistcoat. He was an impressive specimen in showmen terms: oiled bare chest, muscular arms decorated in tattoos and a thick, dark moustache, nestling like a caterpillar above his top lip and seeming all the hairier contrasted against his shaven scalp. He posed and paraded and then, with a matador's flamboyance, The

Mad Maxeman jerked at a red silky cloth.

'Blimey, it's like a butchers shop!' an excited voice shouted from the crowd as knives and axes had been uncovered.

'Goodness gracious! I do hope he's going to be careful with those!' cried out Gertrude Grimshaw who, feeling much better, had joined The Greygoyles at the top of the arena.

'He'll do himself an injury!' said Timothy Grimshaw as The Mad Maxeman hurled the axes aloft.

'So dangerous!' said Emily Gotobed, watching the blades slice the air and looping the loop before he caught them again.

'So dangerous!' repeated 'Old Pugface' Paul Gotobed who was cooling his wife with a hand-held fan.

Timothy Grimshaw who was wigged out as usual and already having a bad day was about to wish that he had stayed at home.

'The man's a lunatic!' he concluded as The Mad Maxeman swung an axe within inches of the crowd.

Suddenly the eagle that had been waiting on its perch for its arena display time swept over the crowd and into the arena. The crowd oohed and ahhed but in a flash the bird was gone, and so, too, was Timothy Grimshaw's wig! The eagle had publicly 'outed' him and the naked truth was there for everyone to see...a shiny pink baldy head that had not felt the sun in years.

'My old fella reckoned Grimshaw wears a rug,' jeered Mikey Mucus bowling his arm and then roaring with laughter as the crowd watched the bird, now back on its perch, rip the wig to shreds.

Pamela Potter swiftly removed a white sun hat from her bag and placed it on Timothy Grimshaw's head without saying a word. The Greygoyles pretended that nothing had happened.

'There's nothing wrong with being bald. Be brave and bin the wig! That's what the bird was trying to tell him,' Tiggy said, for the first time feeling a little bit sorry for a Greygoyle.

'Never had the problem myself,' chuckled Arthur Ramsbottom grabbing his ponytail.

He was glowing so pink that Tiggy couldn't believe people were not staring at him.

However, The Mad Maxeman was determined that the bird would not steal the show.

'Er now let me see. I need two English roses to help me, um....' he announced scanning the crowd

His eyes fell upon Penelope.

'Ah yes! I've found a beautiful Princess! Perfect! And her beautiful mother too!' said the showman taking them both by the hand and leading them into the arena.

'I feel sick!' groaned Tiggy as she watched The Mad Maxeman blindfold and stand them with their backs pressed against a board.

The Mad Maxeman worked the crowd, swinging a woodchopper around and around like a propeller allowing the tension to mount.

'I can't watch!' Tiggy gulped, fixing her eyes onto the metal blade flashing in the sunlight.

The audience held its breath until eventually the showman released the weapon. Arthur Ramsbottom gave Tiggy's clammy palm a comforting squeeze. Blade after blade thudded into the backboard, skimming the silhouettes of mother and daughter. With every impact, the crowd flinched and oohed whilst Tiggy breathed a sigh of relief. Just the space above their heads remained. James Cartwright looked like he was praying.

'The Lord's My Shepherd, I'll not want;

He makes me down to lie.

In pastures green; He leadeth me,' he sang to relieve his tension.

The crowd gasped as the final blade came within a whisker of Alison Tipple's perm and set. The lacquer did its job and not a hair moved but the blade had sailed straight through a gap in Penelope's tiara and when the two 'English roses' walked away, the crown remained pinned to the board. The Mad Maxeman held their hands aloft, milking the audience's applause. Tiggy jumped the cordon and flung her arms around her sister, the crowd spontaneously 'aahing', only for yet another unexpected bonus to follow, one of those special moments that the villagers would talk about for years. Alicia Duncan Forbes, all feet and jewellery, worried about her beautiful suspended tiara had entered the arena.

'Get yer old man to buy ya another!' shouted Mikey Mucus. 'He's loaded!' He turned to Toadie and lowered his voice. 'My old fella reckons he's out with a different dolly bird every week!'

Mikey bowled his arm to point at Alicia Duncan Forbes.

'Not my diamond tiara...anything but my tiara... every stone is genuine...there's houses cost less!' Alicia Duncan Forbes wailed, her gold sovereigns and charm bracelet jangling on her wrists as she shook her diamond-studded fist.

An excited buzz started in the audience. Everyone knew how important the tiara was to the woman.

'You silly man!' shrieked Alicia Duncan Forbes violently battering The Mad Maxeman with her handbag.

The air filled with laughter as the muscle-man legged it out of the arena with an angry Alicia Duncan Forbes at his heels and brandishing an axe in her hand. The journalists from the local press rubbed their hands with glee.

Chapter 16

WINNERS AND LOSERS

The afternoon tea dance had claimed several casualties. Greygoyles in high heels usually ended up in the First Aid tent. Mrs. Gibson hobbled out of the marquee on her husband's arm with her wedge heels in her hand and her bunions throbbing.

'I'm not going to say that I told you so,' he scolded and she scowled back in reply.

Thomas Tipple still 'suited and booted,' and having jobbed his jobs was pacing the exhibition stands. He spotted his name by his entries and puzzled by the curly and blotchy appearance of his runner beans, he immediately suspected an act of sabotage, but the arrival inside the marquee of Lord and Lady Butcher meant that it was all too late to protest. Lord Butcher had been "Mad Eric" for many years. He went everywhere on a hop-along scooter and never wore his false teeth on Wednesdays and Fridays. However, when the chance came up to purchase the title, Eric Butcher had been first in the queue. He had been poor ever since but it had nevertheless bought him overnight respectability. After that, he was Lord Butcher, and the Greygoyle men doffed their caps whenever he passed by on his scooter.

The self-appointed Lord, dressed in his usual tweeds and bow tie, stood on the stage preening his moustache and twiddling its tips to a point. All afternoon he had been trying to lose his strong Norfolk dialect in an attempt to sound posh. His wife, dressed in gaudy polyester and bright red lipstick, applied well beyond her lips natural outline, was holding the envelopes with the prize-winners' names.

A little later, when Alison Tipple, flushed and out-of-breath, entered from a side entrance, several winners were holding trophies with lipstick kiss imprints on their cheeks.

'This study of the English countryside with its glorious poppies completely won our hearts,' read Lord Butcher from the judges notes.

He paused, enjoying the drama and building his part. His wife rustled the envelope containing the winners name under his nose.

'Slow yew down woman!' he said, slipping into

comfortable speech, reluctantly taking it from her. He took a few long, slurpy sips of water. The audience started to fidget. 'The deserving winner of the Open Art Competition,' he paused again to open the envelope.

Alison Tipple titivated her hair and took a small step forward practising her winner's smile.

'Cor blarst me, thass a rummun!' exclaimed the Lord in his broadest Norfolk accent. 'It's that l'il ole gal, Miss Tiggy Tipple!'

Shock waves reverberated around Great Snubington's Art Society, but Tiggy, having bumped into Mrs. Derbyshire by Churchill's pen, was not there to receive her prize. Mrs.D had greeted her with some very hot news: Norman the globetrotting gnome had mysteriously turned up on the tombola stall and Timothy Grimshaw had bought as many tickets as it took to win their 'baby' back again. His wife had promptly fainted only to get carted off to the First Aid tent for the second time that day.

As Mrs. Derbyshire and her young companion approached the marquee, Tiggy once again thought she saw the boy from the woods enter the tent ahead of them. She photographed him with her instamatic, hoping that the sun would not be too bright to see him when the film was eventually processed. Lord Butcher's distinctive voice was bumbling out the various categories and winners.

'And now for the winner of The Knit More Nora Award for The Most Useful Creation category' he said trying to speak with a plum in his mouth. He took the envelope from his wife. 'Hold you hard!' he said drifting back to his natural pre-title strong Norfolk dialect again.

The audience sniggered and whispered as Lord Butcher opened the envelope and hesitated, mouthing the winners name to try to get his posh voice back again.

'Mrs. Alison Tipple,' he announced holding up the winning entry of a knitted doll to hide the spare toilet-roll. 'Thass suffen bootiful!' he declared prompting the audience to burst out laughing.

In Tiggy's opinion, the dolls were more hideous than a toilet roll could ever be. She wondered if the boy was watching, but scanning the rows of seats and the standing hordes he was nowhere to be seen. Tiggy was in fact, so fixed on finding him that she did not even realise that her mother was about to collect the 'Best Home-Made' award for her 'Rustic Raspberry' preserve. Mikey Mucus, ever ready to humiliate, blew a loud raspberry as she stood up which made Toadie laugh so much that he snorted his cola out through his nose.

The gardening awards were a bit like the Hollywood Oscars, everybody being far more interested in the reactions of the losers than they were in the winners. Thomas Tipple, so far not having won a thing, was convinced he was a victim of sabotage. When the next three awards also went to Hattie Hipperson, the woman at the centre of the judge-fixing allegations, the mood was feisty.

'She reckons she had a bee sting on her backside! Pull the other one. It's got bells on!' grumbled Hugo F. Uppingham.

The buzz in the audience had real venom. Thomas Tipple had resigned himself to disappointment. It was just not going to be his year, but then suddenly, above the disgruntled mutters, he heard his name called out like a mantra as he did a clean sweep of the floral categories.

'Thank you, Alex and Orange Realm butterfly! You are life savers!' Tiggy said under her breath remembering what Alex had said about the orange winged visitor to their garden.

The biggest title, Great Snubington's Most Outstanding Garden of the Year' award, had been kept until last. Arthur Ramsbottom was runner up for 'the most spectacular display of sunflowers' that the village had ever seen. There had been a number of horrified gasps.

'Everyone knows he has nettles and thistles. His garden is very weedish,' muttered Terence Tiddy.

'Are the judges blind!' complained Ernest McAvey patting Terence Tiddy's knee.

Nobody had been more surprised than Arthur Ramsbottom. He hobbled away, smothered in Lady Butcher's lipstick and winked at Tiggy as he put the trophy in her lap. She wished the mysterious boy from the woods had seen but he didn't seem to be in the marquee any more. Lord Butcher poured himself another glass of water, taking several long sips as the tension continued to build. Moments later, it was Thomas Tipple with Lady Butcher's lipstick kisses on his cheek, but this time he was so happy he didn't remove it. There was a real danger a bottle of fizzy Pomagne would be cracked open at Pearly Gates later that evening to celebrate the achievements in style.

Chapter 17

THE YELLOW REALM

The next morning the Pearly Gates mantelpiece gleamed with new trophies and Alison Tipple with a real girly spring to her step was unable to stop smiling. In almost forty years of living life in the beige, listening to other peoples' stories and claims to fame, Alison Tipple, thanks to The Mad Maxeman finally had one of her very own to tell.

It had been an eventful breakfast; Penelope had accidentally sprinkled salt on her grapefruit and Alex, having broken house rules, had kept his trainers on indoors. It was to spiral completely out of control when Tiggy tied his laces together beneath the table. Alex had then tripped, sending a piece of hotly-buttered, jammy toast flying through the air and it had speared itself on their mother's spiky curlers and been left hanging. To crown it all, Thomas Tipple having been too hasty with his crumpet had burped over the Spring Bouquet tablecloth, and yet for once, Alison Tipple did not mind. In fact, she was in such a good mood that Penelope seized the moment.

'Do you think we could get a dog? We'd love a puppy!' she said looking her mother straight in the eye.

Alex and Tiggy nodded in support.

'Please!' Tiggy pleaded.

Alison Tipple didn't get angry but her response was no surprise.

'You know they smell 'doggy' and drop hair everywhere! Please no asking me again! You know it is ridiculous!'

The family calendar for the week ahead read 'Photographer (to be confirmed), Haircuts, Nails and Wax.' Sharon, the village Avon lady, mobile hairdresser and makeover queen was due at Pearly Gates to perform, in Tiggy's opinion, "all manner of gruesome deeds." Tiggy always dreaded it but was determined to have a good day regardless of what else the week had in store.

The weather was t-shirt warm with perfect blue skies, brilliant sunshine and cauliflower cotton wool clouds that were so well defined that it was as if a child, or Alison Tipple, had drawn them. Tiggy glimpsed her father's suit and tie exercising his green fingers in the rustic wigwam. He was 'jobbing a job' with a quick purge before work. The robin was there again.

'It's great to win but now people will be looking harder than ever to see if we've got weeds,' he said.

Net curtains were on the move as Tiggy cycled down the close. At Number 11, the blinds were open and Ernest McAvey and Terence Tiddy, still in their dressing gowns, were looking out of their living room window. The two men had their arms around each other but spotting Tiggy on her bicycle they quickly separated and waved to her, even though they wouldn't normally do so. She had seen the entire little episode and the fact that they had waved to her seemed the strangest thing out of it all.

Tiggy cycled on past the Grimshaws' fortress of recently installed burglar alarm, padlocks and chained gateways. Dartanian, their new guard dog, still hadn't learnt to bark. It was such a dopey dog but at least Norman was back fishing in the ornamental rock pool even if there were no fish. Tiggy had loved the idea of a great mystery to solve. For a few days, Norman's disappearance had made Heavenly Gardens more interesting but that was before her rainbow adventures and her encounter with the stranger in the woods. These things now owned her mind and thoughts, drawing her back again. In fact, she could think of nothing else and had started to record it all in a brand-new diary that she had never intended to use.

"Diaries are for bores and people with secrets. I am not a bore but I do have a secret. A very big one: I have rainbow power and The Stig Man is teaching me how to use it. Then I will get rid of The Greygoyles and all other bad, boring stuff..... like diaries. The Orange Realm is awesome. It's about saying 'I can' and not 'I can't.' The baby bird turned into an eagle when it believed it could fly. It came to the Fun Day and ripped up Mr. Grimshaw's wig. Mr.G should be bald and proud.

I won a book voucher and a paintbrush for my pic of Mrs.D's Mum says it is posh 'cos the hairy bit you paint with is made of sable. Alex says sable like that comes from the tail of a weasel. That is not posh, it's cruel, so I won't use it!

Mr. Sheepsbottom says I should keep the trophy for his garden award 'cos my sunflowers were the reason he won. Father won loads. Alex says he's knuckle-walking like a silverback gorilla but father doesn't know that his wins are down to Alex and The Orange Realm butterfly.

Found out there is a lot of yucky, gross stuff in The Indigo. When it is my time to go I will ask The Stig Man to come with me. He really misses Ashwin, his brother Josh and peanut-

butter and jelly sandwiches. His dreadlocks are ace but Mum would say he looks like a hippy.

Nadia Commonetchy, (can't spell it) is a gymnastics queen. So many perfect scores she's now called 'Little Miss Perfect.' Nobody is perfect but girls can be winners too, so there! Pen and me have been doing cartwheels everywhere we go.

P.S. Mrs.D is sad that the curse got Mr. Dodds. Mum says that his brushes were not much use anyway but she will miss his dusters. I saw Mr. Uppingham picking his nose in his car again. Stupid man must think nobody can see him....and he thinks he's posh! Duh! I shall call him 'The Bogey Man!'

P.P.S. We have a friendly robin in the garden. Alex says robins are dead people in disguise. He says it might be 'nice Grandma' or Mr.D paying us a visit so I mustn't scare it away. I am just so worried it might get Sluggy and Huggy and I have no idea what to do."

In the meadows, butterflies fluttered, poppies and daisies were dancing as the air, thick with pollen, tickled inside Tiggy's nose. Her mouth was sugar coated from a left-over Fun Day doughnut she had eaten without licking her lips. It was all a part of her will power and stamina training. She sped down the track, past the lightning tree, not daring to give it even a glance, and onto the Derbyshires' yard. Churchill was in his pen but today she did not stop, pedalling even more vigorously as the mill came into view. The puddle was even bigger and swerving to avoid the water, Tiggy took a detour around the back of the mill. The Boggle's barrel was there in its usual spot and so, too, up to her waist in water was a young girl who she had never seen before.

'Mind you don't wake up The Boggle!' called out Tiggy, still sat astride her bicycle. 'He's always asleep at this time of day. Mr.D told me that.' Tiggy stared at the girl cowering in her boyish clothes and clumpy boots.

'S...s...s...so...sorry,' stammered the girl stepping clear of the water whilst holding on to a straw boater preventing it from slipping off her head.

'How come you're not wet?' asked Tiggy noticing that the girl was curiously dry.

Suddenly the barrel toppled over into the puddle, bobbing violently upon the water.

'Boggle! Don't worry I'll save you!' shouted Tiggy, her bike splashing into the water so she could steady the barrel.

The world around her began spinning like a top and for a moment, everything was a blur until she was on her ghost bike soaring high into the sky and rainbow bound once more.

Tiggy had stopped spinning and was floating into a downward spiral, the ghost bike free falling in slow motion, as if suspended by an invisible parachute into the golden light of a maze. Although she didn't know it she was about to plunge deep into The Yellow Realm of the rainbow. Tiggy breathed deeply to stay calm but the ghost bike, unlike when it was her normal **BMX**, was now in control of her. The further she fell the more an image of the Wobniar was appearing beneath her, similar to a crop circle down on earth. At first it was clear and detailed but the closer she got to the golden maze, the more the contours blurred until definition was completely lost. However, the individual elements came into sharper focus. There were thousands of daffodils making up the circle. The golden trumpet of every flower became distinct and real.

'What an incredible place!' Tiggy said clinging on tightly to Pirate Pants as they touched down into The Realm. 'Maybe we'll see The Stig Man,' she whispered as they wandered between the trunk-like stems.

These were shadow lands where there was no colour until looking up at the gloriously yellow trumpets towering high above. It was as if a mythical Sun God had dipped them in liquid gold and blessed them. Sure enough, The Book of The Realms was there and so, too, was The Stig Man, waiting for her. After their Special Buddy hand greeting, The Stig Man caught up on all The Fun Day news.

'You don't like that Alicia woman do you, Girlie! She

sounds horrific!' The Stig Man said, grinning as Tiggy pretended to vomit.

Suddenly, The Book of The Realms began to glow like golden sunshine.

'Talk of the devil,' said Tiggy as an image of Alicia Duncan Forbes appeared upon the page.

Her own mother was there, too, with her 'House Sitters' Roster' in her trembling hand. A cloud of rainbow dust sprinkled onto a daffodil trumpet and one by one, the petals turned to yellow crystals before their eyes.

'My Mum was brave to do that when she was so scared,' said Tiggy running her fingers through the crystals that were fine like on a sugar doughnut. 'Her courage is the positive energy that made these crystals.'

Tiggy looked for confirmation.

'You're getting super smart, Miss Tiggy! You're working it out for yourself,' said The Stig Man like a proud parent. 'So, what d'ya think is negative energy in this Realm for your quest, Miss Tiggy?'

'I think it must be being chicken.'

The American boy hesitated.

'A cowardy custard?' Tiggy added to alter the boy's blank expression.

'You sure have some funny talk in your vocab. Miss Tiggy, but if you mean being a scaredy cat then you're bang on!' he said with a grin.

The Book of The Realms pulsated and Angel Seraphina's hologram appeared once more.

'Awh! Sacred Secret time already,' said Tiggy with a deep sigh.

Both children knew that it was time for her to go solo and their time together had been all too brief.

The Book of The Realms had revealed Tiggy's quest. She climbed up the trunk-like stem and into the giant daffodil's silky-smooth trumpet. Tiggy felt small and insignificant inside the giant flower, staring into the golden tunnel that stretched out before her as far as the eye could see. Here in the trumpet's tunnel her skin looked like it was bathed in butter, the golden child that her mother had always wanted her to be. Powdered stamens the size of cricket bats were obstacles to her quest although she had no clear idea of what she was doing there except that she was to find and save an Elfibub. She felt sure that even Alex did not know what an Elfibub looked like, but she trusted she was about to find out. Just as the unknown can be scary for anyone, trepidation gripped her tight or at least it did until she discovered a tiny cute creature with a bubble body and elfish ears peeping out from behind a stamen. Tiggy knew that this was the Elfibub, her anxiety melting immediately at the sweet desperation of the endearing creature before her. The Elfibub's body, especially its ears, were shivering and quaking.

'I daren't do it!' squeaked the Elfibub in a high-pitched voice like it had swallowed a mouthful of helium, and its pointy ears trembled even more. 'I'm not brave enough to steal the sting from a bee in the honeycomb.'

The Elfibub pointed into the tunnel for her to look. Tiggy could see something glistening gold in the distance.

'I can't do it, but I'll be banished to The Indigo as a Beezelfibub if I don't ...cowards always do...it's the bad energy,' added the creature, 'I'm so scared.'

Angel Seraphina gave Tiggy an encouraging squeeze. She instantly felt a surge of courage and overwhelming desire to help the Elfibub. It drove her down the trumpet's tunnel until she came to the honeycomb.

The buzzing was deafening when Tiggy reached the labyrinth and the instant she stepped inside she could taste the sticky sweetness in every breath. The bees droned and the honey dripped. She licked a drop off her lips and the sweetness melted upon her tongue, a taste so distinctively delicious it could have been nectar sent from The Gods. The hostile bees angrily swarmed around her. She was an unwelcome and uninvited guest, but still buoyed up with courage from Angel Seraphina's reassuring presence Tiggy did not feel afraid. A bee came near and she snatched at its velvet suit circling the tip of her nose but it stung a moment before she caught it. Normally it would have hurt but shocked by the sudden explosion of the honeycomb labyrinth the pain was numbed. Golden crystals rained down upon her, a mass of pretty sparkles showering the Rainbow Child from top to toe, one of them falling into Tiggy's hand.

Another realm conquered, Tiggy's courage received its reward with a yellow rainbow stone. Having left the Derbyshire's mill behind, her nose was throbbing from the bee sting but Tiggy knew that it had been worth it. She had saved the little Elfibub from exile to The Indigo.

Chapter 18

"ANY CUT
BUT HALF CUT"

At twenty minutes past four, Sharon of "Any Cut but Half Cut" pulled up in her customised convertible into the Tipples' driveway. Tiggy watched out of the window as Sharon topped up her lip gloss, dusted her nose, fluffed up her feathered flicked out hair, and after one final pout in the mirror, tottered up the path in the highest silver platform shoes that Tiggy had ever seen. She couldn't help but think what hard work it was to be Sharon, or even 'Cherie,' because the hairdresser had an identical twin. Nobody could tell them apart. The mobile business was a joint operation and between them, they cut and styled nearly every head of hair in the village.

The hairdresser was running late, a blue rinse with a pinky-tinge and a nit infestation in the old part of the village had been to blame.

'What a day, babe!' said Sharon as Alison Tipple welcomed the hairdresser at the door. 'It's that dreadful Nightingale Road again…I got to number 64 like, to be greeted by a frantic mother and five kids, each with a head full of nits. I told her straight, I don't do nits, babe, but before I knew it like, she'd locked the door behind me. The next thing I know like, the kids are giving the nits pet names and racing them on the kitchen table. I tell ya babe, it was so disgusting, I nearly puked!'

Alison Tipple winced and took a sidelong glance at the hairdresser's collection of brushes and combs, hoping they were not contaminated. Thomas Tipple having arrived home especially early from work, loosened his tie and went straight to the front of the queue. Sharon could have cut his hair blindfolded having had the same short back and sides ever since he was a boy.

'I reckon like, you ought to be a bit more adventurous like, babe,' said the hairdresser, as she flashed the clippers across the nape of his neck. 'Try it a bit longer like, and grow some side burns. It's all the rage like. You could really rock a mullet, babe!'

She paused looking him right in the eyes. Thomas Tipple jittered on his seat.

'Even at your age!' she said running her hands through his hair.

Thomas Tipple blushed. The hairdresser had a reputation in the village as being 'a bit of a girl with the men.' In Sharon's world 'monogamy' was a kind of dark coloured wood and life was too short for a long-term relationship when 'long' stood for anything over a month. She was a self-confessed dating addict and would be the first to admit that she was not fussy about her men.

'As long as he has a pulse like and is on the cool side of fifty like, I'll give him a try,' Sharon told any customer listening to her dating adventures. 'Of course, it helps if he's rich and handsome like, but, like, I'm not fussed as long as he can pay the bill!'

Thomas Tipple hoped that the village 'man-eater' was not making a move on him and sat for the rest of the hair-cut with his eyes glued to the floor until he could safely declare that his haircut was 'another job jobbed.'

Tiggy was quietly suffering from her bee sting and could have done without being 'Sharonned' today. Not only did her nose look crimson and swollen but it throbbed like mad as well. To make matters worse, her mother was cross for having to postpone the photographer for the family's annual sitting.

'We can hardly send out Christmas photo cards with

this one looking like a clown!' Alison Tipple complained to the hairdresser.

'Ahh babe, you poor baby...bless!' comforted Sharon, rubbing Tiggy on her shoulder.

'I always think you can tell so much about a person by the card they send you,' said Alison.

'Yeah, how much they like you,' added Sharon. 'You can always tell like, when you've got the naff card from the bottom of the box! Hate it like when twinny's is better, or I get a robin card. Straight in the bin!' she continued 'right gives me the creeps, like. I don't want any dead person like, visiting me, thanks babe!'

Tiggy couldn't wait for Sharon to be done with her. She didn't care how hideous she looked but her nose felt like it was going to explode and the sight of it was making her mother increasingly irritable. Even if Tiggy could have explained about saving the Elfibub, she knew that her mother would neither have believed nor excused her.

Alex had been dreading his turn and sat down fidgeting like he had an army of ants in his pants, itching to escape from the hairdresser's chair and what he described as her 'widiculous conversation.'

'Girlfwiends!' grumbled Alex checking out his unfashionably short haircut in the hall mirror.

'You look like a coconut!' Tiggy said beginning to giggle and dropping the book she had been balancing on her head whilst using her new clackers.

'Girlfwiends!' Alex repeated. 'It's all she ever asks me about….as if I'm into all that shenanigans….do I look like a walking hormone? Alex scoffed. 'What a stupid woman! Even worse still, she comes in duplicate. Her twin is a wight dipstick as well,' he said loitering a while to eavesdrop for cheap entertainment.

Back in the kitchen was a full-on bitch fest. Alison Tipple in her staid twinset and Sharon in her plunging neck line and figure-hugging flares would have seemed an unlikely couple to hit it off, but they did. Appearances were very important to both of them and so they got each other and were totally on the same page about nails, home catalogues, perfumes and other 'smellies.' Hair and make-up, facials, manicure and pedicure - Sharon and Cherie did the lot and had plans to branch out into aromatherapy and massage.

'When I first heard about 'essential oils,' before I got myself educated like, I was worried sick…they're 'essential' like, and yet we hadn't got any. Oh babe, you would have laughed…I convinced myself that one night I would go to bed like, and not wake up. What am I like, babe…mad or what?' said the hairdresser laughing and rolling up a curler. Alex shook his head in disbelief.

'Definitely mad but for once, actually wight! Of course, one day she won't wake up when there's a last time for everwything for everwyone! Fact!' said Alex muttering something about the 'Suffwagettes dying for Shawon to have the vote,' as he went upstairs to avoid further irritation.

Alison Tipple's hairstyle was like candy floss. It looked like it might be soft but it felt stiff and scratchy from the lashings of lacquer and Tiggy hated touching it. Sharon knew exactly how Alison Tipple liked her hair and as she created a nest upon the woman's head, her client gave a dramatic account of her close encounter with the Mad Maxeman's axe. However, it didn't take long for the pair to get onto one of their favourite subjects, namely the very striking Madeleine Beau Ellison, Sharon having recently seen her in the chemists buying a nit treatment shampoo and comb.

'You should have seen her at The Fun Day! Dripping in make-up and in a most vulgar dress,' Alison Tipple said checking out Sharon's cheesecloth blouse that had been buttoned just enough to be very revealing. 'She made a right show of herself!'

'Sounds well tarty does that, babe!' said Sharon frowning, having noticed a chip in one of her new red finger nails. 'Oh f....fudge! Bang goes my date.' She inspected the damage. 'Just have to stay in like, and fix these nails. Twinny can go instead. The guy'll never know!'

Alison Tipple was stunned but quite envied how Sharon took life in its stride and really didn't care about what anyone thought of her.

Anyway, where were we babe?' asked the hairdresser, keen to continue the bitching. Tiggy who was eavesdropping in the hall found the conversation strange.

'Are they bonkers? Madeleine Beau Ellison is so beautiful. She's amazing!' she mumbled, moving the elegant goddess-like figurine off its mat on the hall table. It had always reminded her of Madeleine.

'Isn't it terrible about Dave Dodds?' continued Sharon satisfied they had verbally destroyed the village beauty. 'I must confess like, I had a rather awkward date with him once. Hate to say it like, but it felt more like being out with my granddad! I feel bad like, for calling him "Oddsy Doddsy" now!'

'You weren't to know,' responded Alison checking out her new hairdo in Sharon's mirror.'

'Everyone says the curse got him,' said Sharon rolling her eyes and smirking. 'If you believe in it, like. Not that I do.'

Alison Tipple could feel herself getting very hot and took out her purse to pay. Sharon however, was far more interested in talking about the curse.

'It was twins that started it all. They were boys about your Tiggy's age. Struck by lightning, they were like. Bless!' said Sharon refusing to take the money not to wind things up. 'Apparently, there's a tree on the

Derbyshire's land where it happened. On your doorstep nearly, like.'

Alison Tipple shuddered. 'You shouldn't talk about it!' she said waving a pound note at her.

Sharon burst out laughing.

'Oh babe! Do you really believe that ol' nonsense! Bit late anyway. I've been chatting about it like, all day in every house I've been, like,' she said staring at the money.

Alison Tipple looked shocked and pale.

'Are you alright, babe?' asked Sharon putting some hair clippings in the bin.

'Please stop talking about it!' said Alison Tipple giving up on paying and sweeping the hair up off the floor.

'Nah! It's all fine! Besides like, it can't tell me from my twinny!' said Sharon, thinking she was hilarious. 'Which reminds me, I've still got bottles and bottles of cleaning stuff like, that Dave gave me in the back of my cupboards and I haven't used a drop. Perhaps I'll give it a go to show my respect like.'

When Tiggy arrived at Alex's room for her daily lecture, he was laying on his bed singing to Bowie's 'Life on Mars' that was playing on his record player. His stamp album was open on the bed and he was updating his 'Tipple's Almanac' with fresh predictions: Beverly Ramsbottom would quit the cruise ships for a convent,

Alicia Duncan Forbes would undergo revolutionary treatment to have her feet downsized, the curse would be no more and the Tipples themselves, would have a puppy and have moved house by Christmas.

'I needed to escape Bungalow Sha.' mumbled Alex without looking up.

'What did you just call her?' asked Tiggy.

'Bungalow Sha.... because she has nothing upstairs!' he replied touching his head.

'We can't all be a smart Alex, now can we babe,' mocked Tiggy perfectly mimicking the hairdresser's unrefined accent.

'You missed out the 'like!' jibed Alex, but still finding his sister funny. 'Hey, clown features, how's your konk? Is it thwobbing?' he asked wincing at the sight of her nose.

'Killer!' replied Tiggy. She looked at herself in his mirror and tentatively touched it as if she thought it would drop off.

'You never told us how or where it happened,' said Alex, laying down his notebook.

'That's top secret and if I told you I might just have to kill you,' Tiggy jested hitting Alex repeatedly with a pillow until he retaliated.

Shrieks of laughter filled the room but a small slit in the seam of Alex's battle pillow eventually made them stop at the sight of feathers flying everywhere.

'Okay! So, what's it to be today, Tig?' asked Alex, frantically stuffing the feathers back inside the pillow.

'Rainbows. Tell me everything you know about them. There was an ace one this morning. Did you see it?' Tiggy enquired, trying to sound very matter of fact so as not to arouse suspicion.

'Impossible sis....you never get wainbows on days like this....ask any meteowologist and they will tell you the same. Weflection, wefwaction and dispersion of light in water dwoplets that wesult in a spectwum of light appeawing in the sky. Seven colours awwanged in an arc and a pot of gold at its end. Believe that and you must believe anything!' he said, removing a book off the shelf.

Tiggy looked at her brother with suspicion. Alex was the cleverest person she knew but he must be wrong about this. She was bursting to challenge him and tell him more about the rainbow that morning but she knew what had happened to The Stig Man. He had said too much and now he would probably never go home.

The Indigo dilemma of whether to go or not to go had been weighing on Tiggy's mind and had been a burden to her happiness every time she had returned from another rainbow adventure. She knew that it would be a decision that she alone would have to make and probably quite soon. She trusted Alex with all her heart and wondered whether he might know how dangerous it would be.

A storm had been brewing for most of the day and by bed time it was ready to rumble. Tiggy couldn't sleep, tossing and turning as the hollow beats of the wooden wind chime, hanging from the apple tree outside her bedroom window, kept her awake. She thought about what Alex had told her about rainbows and how he suspected that she might be an 'Indigo Child' because she got bored so easily and disliked it when people told her what to do. He had said that not being able to sleep was also a sign. Tiggy wrestled with her tangled sheets, unable to switch off from thinking about the boy and girl at the mill. She hoped that they were safe and as she snuggled up to Pants her thoughts eventually journeyed back to the land of unicorns and angels.

Tiggy had only just dropped off to sleep when she woke to a loud clap of thunder. She tuck-rolled out of bed and pulled back her bedroom curtain. Much needed rain now pounded against the glass and between the distant rolls of thunder, she listened to the wind. It had dropped a little but it sounded creepy now, like a kitten crying for its mother. She opened her window to listen, worrying about the mill children once more. Another roll of thunder and a bird began to sing and the security light from next door unexpectedly came on, illuminating her sleeping sunflowers in the neighbours' garden and a robin flapping its wings around the light. However, much more surprisingly, Arthur Ramsbottom was there too. He was standing with his stick in the pouring rain, his long silver hair hanging freely as she had never seen it before. Tiggy watched intently from her darkened room as the man raised his stick to the sky. At that moment, a fork of lightning flashed lighting up her neighbour. Arthur Ramsbottom was only wearing pyjamas. He must have been soaked to the skin but he stood there for several minutes gazing up into the night sky as a rosy glow surrounded him. Tiggy grabbed her camera and fired off three shots at him, but in the dark she felt sure that nothing would come out, although the rosy glow was certainly very bright. Arthur Ramsbottom stayed a while until he hobbled indoors and the light went off, leaving the neighbour's garden in darkness. Tiggy noticed that another light was on in the 'Jobs been jobbed shed.'

'Father's not going to be pleased about that,' she mumbled and before going back to bed, Tiggy made a note by torchlight to remember to tell him in the morning.

Chapter 19

THE LIBRARY

Tiggy's diary was lying open on her desk.

Monday 26th July

"I got the yellow crystal. Woohoo! A stupid bee stung my nose. It hurts more than Mikey's Chinese wrist burns, but Mum doesn't care and called me a 'la la baby.' I hate it when she does that. Alex thinks I am an 'Indigo Child.' This might help me in The Indigo if I dare do it.

P.S. Sharon's white flares and silver platforms look silly! She looks like she is at a disco."

Tiggy took her pen, turning to a fresh page and began to write.

Tuesday 27th July

'Mr. Sheepsbottom has funny pjs with a groovy pattern. The fashion police will arrest him if they find out. It is weird how he is glowing bright pink. It may be too much candy floss or that Ready Brek cereal stuff that makes kids glow on the T.V. advert. I will ask Alex and find out what Mr. Sheepsbottom has for breakfast.'

The days following the storm had been eventful. The next morning Tiggy had returned to the mill to check up on the mill children. She suspected that they had been sleeping inside and that such torrential rain could only serve to drive them away. However, her anxiety settled when she found that the puddle strangely had not got any bigger.

Tiggy had spent many hours trying to master the perfect Superman and on these visits had met up with the mill children, who together she had affectionately named 'The Millies.' The boy was Millie A and the girl was Millie B in the order that she had met them. Recently, they had seemed happier than usual and she had even taken their photos although both had seemed a little camera shy. They had explored the woods and made hideouts together, her time with them finishing with another amazing visit on her ghost bike to the rainbow.

Tiggy now had a crystal from the green rainbow realm to add to her collection. She treasured this rainbow gift but above all, she prized her very special friendship with The Stig Man. They had had so much fun together and had shared so many special moments that she did not ever want to forget.

'I guess diaries do have their uses,' she told Pants as she took her pen to write it all down to strengthen her memory in the days to come.

Saturday 7th August

"What an amazing adventure! In The Green Realm, we had four seasons in just one afternoon. The Stig Man (who is now officially my and Pants' best friend) buried himself in leaves and pounced on me. It made me jump so bad he cried laughing. He is so right about feelings. They can be very destructive, even deadly and is the reason The Indigo is so scary. It is a sin bin of evil thoughts and feelings. The Stig Man (coolest boy ever except for Alex) says each realm gets rid of its own poison there. I learnt so much in The Green Realm and I am starting to understand it all. I loved The Greengrunger Karma Charmas. They are peace-loving and so free spirited. The Stig Man says they are 'the coolest dudes in the rainbow' that live and let

live and disagree with envy. Envy is toxic! Bad stuff like that belongs in The Indigo. That's why The Bitch Queen (Alicia Duncan Forbes) and Emily Gotobed hate each other, because they are jealous of each other's jewellery. The Book of The Realms proved it. There was so much black dust that we couldn't even see each other. Leaf kicking with The Green Grungers was fun but the tree hugging was a bit weird. I think they must be big nature lovers because their clothes are made of leaves. They looked so cute in their acorn hats. My favourite bit was doing the maze with The Stig Man. We were trying to find The Green Man but then I lost The Stig Man and got lost, too. A green dragonfly showed me the way. I think Angel Seraphina guided me to follow it 'cos then it was easy to find The Green Man. I think he is sort of The Green Realm's boss. He is soooo bossy! He made me pick up every single oak leaf and acorn. There were thousands of them! It turned out that it was my Rainbow Quest test. I had to show enough patience and when I picked up the very last acorn, it turned into the green crystal that I needed. It was a pity that The Stig Man didn't see me get it."

The trapped Rainbow Child was her rock, a trusted and giving companion who had selflessly helped her through her travels. He had given answers and solutions to her many problems despite his own desperate plight. The poor boy was stuck there with a rebellious punk angel who was getting hairier by the day.

It had also been a summer of visits to Mrs. Derbyshire's farm. Tiggy would have loved telling Mrs. D about the rainbow and the funny goings-on at the mill but she knew they had to remain a secret and she had locked it away inside her heart. Shame really, Mrs. Derbyshire would have believed her story. She always did. However, on a positive, her parents not finding out had to be a plus because even as it was, they were both acting far stranger than usual. Over recent days her father had spent more and more time in his shed, less time jobbing jobs and he had replaced his being clean shaven obsession with pork chop sideburns and stubble. Her mother was in serious meltdown over the tragic news that Sharon's twin sister, Cherie, was now the 14th victim of the curse. It was a fatal road accident, Cherie swerving to avoid a deer and crashing into a tree. Nobody else was involved. Alison Tipple felt responsible for Sharon talking about the curse when she visited just a couple of days before the crash. She even blamed herself for not having cancelled the hairdresser when she had postponed the photographer because she minded about Tiggy's red nose. The way she saw it, was that she was the catalyst for this series of unfortunate events, and Sharon could easily not have been there that day to talk about the wretched curse. Her anxiety and upset was making her do all sorts of weird stuff. Well, weird stuff for her that is. She had started to wear trousers and had not even once enquired, 'does my bottom look big in this?' In fact, her choice of clothing was strikingly more masculine and although she still knitted, she would only use black wool. She was making a set of clothes for Pants of all things. It seemed like she wanted any excuse to hold the bear and keep him close to her for a while. Tiggy was in no doubt that her parents were troubled and it felt like it was from something beyond their control. They were going through the motions of presenting themselves as a 'normal couple' with 'normal' children by Greygoyle standards, and yet neither of them really believed it. There was something fake about it all and their need to fit in. Heavenly Gardens had made owning fancy shoes important when they never had been before. Tiggy wondered whether it could be to do with their age since she had heard about how turning forty could send people cranky. That was probably it. Furthermore, things took a turn for the worse when Tiggy arrived home late for dinner and had accidentally left a freshly moulded chewing gum monster on a kitchen chair and her mother had sat on it.

'Wretched girl! Now look what you've made me do!' Alison Tipple yelled, peeling the gooey mess from the back of her trousers. 'My first ever pair of bell bottoms absolutely ruined! I only ordered them from my catalogue last month!'

'Awh! You've flattened Mr. Tiddy!' said Tiggy looking at what was left of her monster.

'Forget Mr. Tiddy! You're grounded for the week!' snarled Alison Tipple, throwing what was left of him in gum form, into the bin and storming out of the room.

'Reckon I did her a favour!' mumbled Tiggy under her breath. 'Those trousers were hideous!'

Tiggy was stuck at Pearly Gates going up the walls with boredom. Therefore, when it was time for their compulsory fortnightly trip to the library, she was happy to go for the first time ever, just to get out somewhere. These outings were her parents' idea of family fun. They all went and just as holidays were added to a family calendar, these visits, too, were marked in red as for all other important events.

On this particular library day, Penelope, who dreamed of being a ballerina, (but dared not admit it because of her father's thing about the odds) had turned down a friend's invitation to The Russian Ballet.

'You can't be in two places at once, Penelope. You have books to choose!' declared her mother, unmoved by her daughter's disappointment, and that was that.

Alex however, was a bookworm. He had been looking forward to the visit ever since returning from the previous trip, whilst Tiggy had already resigned herself to a week of intense boredom.

The library on the outskirts of the nearest town was a favourite haunt of The Greygoyles and on any given day, at least a few of them would be there. The building had originally been the old cottage hospital, but despite Greygoyle petitions and protests against the closure, the hospital continued its life as a library. There were still a few reminders of its past: A pair of old-fashioned scales, the desk from the nurse's station and a wall chart of the human heart. In the foyer, a mock skeleton dressed up with items of lost property guarded the door. It had been wearing a Spider Man bobble hat and one pink mitten since last winter waiting for their owners to claim them.

'All the same old rubbish toys!' said Tiggy glancing into the library toy box and seeing the shape sorter missing most of its shapes and a 'stacking tower' with only two cups.

Penelope gestured for Tiggy to be quiet. She knew what was likely to happen.

'And these are way out of date!' said Tiggy not taking the hint and picking up a pile of Jackie and Bunty comics.

'Ssshh!' came a chorus of disgruntled Greygoyles

sat just the other side of the door.

They looked annoyed. Tiggy shuddered. The building's past gave her the creeps. She hated hospitals and it may have been psychological, but to her the place still reeked of antiseptic. Adding a few Greygoyles to the mix made her nightmare complete. Their numbers were down. Only the 'just good friends' Ernest McAvey and Terence Tiddy along with William Potter, Hugo F. Uppingham and James Cartwright were present, and the latter didn't really count since he was simply planning his own funeral. He did it most weeks.

'Do you think that today will be my last time in this library?' he enquired.

'Probably not!' replied William Potter getting up to escape a morbid conversation.

He was wearing Jesus sandals, the dark patches on his ankle socks making it obvious that his feet were sweaty. However, he was there to make notes and be useful on that helpful neighbour basis and so the cheesy smell was tolerated. A newspaper was on the table. The front page was a picture of Mr. Dodds and Cherie beneath the headline "Village in mourning as curse strikes for the second time in days."

James Cartwright couldn't take his eyes off it.

'Do you think they'll have more people at their funeral than me?' They ignored him. 'Curse victims do well with attendance but I hope I get more,' he said still staring at the newspaper. 'This certainly won't have helped,' he grumbled burying the paper beneath a pile of books so that no other library goers would see it.

Terence Tiddy and Ernest McAvey, wearing black armbands, shook their heads in disbelief. They were playing 'footsie' with each other and their 'pinkies' stayed joined under the table all the time they researched their legal rights regarding some trees planted by their neighbours.

'Firish, evergreenish trees will rob us of all our light,' whispered Terence Tiddy.

William Potter made a note.

'I think legally it's a tricky one,' said Hugo F. Uppingham in a hushed posh voice. Looking at the case law I'd say ask them nicely to dig them up and replace with something more 'airy' if they feel they must. If being reasonable doesn't work, then sue!' he concluded stroking his signature cravat and looking very smug.

Head of this, chair of that, treasurer of the other and all-round busy body, Tiggy thought him a right 'pain in the neck.' The laid-back Luvvies had only planted the saplings a few days prior and would have been shocked if they had known the uproar that their metre high trees had caused.

Alison Tipple having already rehearsed being pleased to see them was unaware that her youngest daughter was behind her holding her nose.

'It's those feet that should be illegal!' whispered Tiggy to her sister.

The library was Alex's idea of 'Heaven on Earth' and he already had an armful of books for himself and was now helping everyone else to choose theirs. He handed Tiggy an Enid Blyton adventure paperback.

'It needs to be bigger!' Tiggy said loudly to annoy The Greygoyles and turning her back on William Potter who put his finger to his mouth to tell her to be quiet.

'I want it to hide this!' she said showing Alex a cycling tricks and stunts guide. 'And it has to pass mum's 'sensible' rule.'

Tiggy scanned the shelves until she found one on crystals and another on the meaning of dreams. She had been having so many unusual dreams lately that a book like this could be useful in case they had an important message to help her with her rainbow quest.

Alex was in his element because Penelope was floundering. She couldn't make up her mind and so Alex did it for her. 'Digging for Fossils' was an unusual choice for a budding ballerina who didn't like to get her hands dirty, but Penelope didn't mind. There was, however, one book still missing from Alex's 'Got to get' book list. 'Rocket Science for Bright Sparks,' had been collecting dust for months and now only the space of the empty kind occupied the shelf. Alex was still moaning about it on the way home.

'Some nerd beat you to it so deal with it!' teased Tiggy, her brother pulling a face back at her.

In all probability the bickering would have continued but for the sight of an unlikely couple on the roadside. Madeleine Beau Ellison had her arm around Lord Butcher.

'That woman's such a flirt!' said Alison Tipple checking herself out in the sun visor's mirror.

'Mad Eric' had in fact recently traded his hop-along scooter for a skateboard. He was not at all good at it and kept wobbling off the board and falling into the road, unaware of any danger. The village beauty was struggling to keep him upright.

'Nits!' Alison Tipple tutted.

'I can't see anything wrong with her ti...' commented Thomas Tipple, mishearing his wife and stopping himself short.

The children gasped; Alison Tipple glared. If looks could kill Thomas Tipple would have died at the wheel, and for the remainder of the journey not another word exchanged between them.

Chapter 20

THE ATTIC

Over the next few days, a heavy cloud affected the mood of the Tipple household. It brought out the worst in the parents and the best in the children. They teamed together, respectful of house rules and sensitive to every nuance of emotion. Outside it was overcast, Tiggy's sunflowers in the next door's garden, with their petals crumpled and fading, reflected the gloominess inside. This sort of dreary day always brought out the best in a Greygoyle who, glad of something to moan about, always found weather like this to be such a bonus, but Tiggy didn't like it. To make matters worse, a mole had run amok in Thomas Tipple's garden overnight and now there were molehills everywhere. Moles were bad news to Thomas Tipple, but equally Thomas Tipple was bad news to moles.

'He's fuming! Penelope said looking out of the window at her father still in his pyjamas jumping up and down on a molehill.

'The little horwors have caused carnage!' Alex said putting on his jelly shoes to help.

'Poor little things!' murmured Tiggy watching as the pyjama-clad duo 'jobbed the job.'

Her father could be brutal and brandishing a shovel above his head, he yelled like a karate black belt before bringing the metal blade crashing down.

'That's another job jobbed!' he yelled triumphantly, every mound of soil having been flattened to a pancake. Twenty minutes later three mole traps were in position. 'That will teach them!' said Thomas Tipple with a smirk.

Thursday 12th August

'My new green crystal is my fave. The Stig Man says that one day we Rainbow Kids will rule the world. We have our own secret handshake called 'The Special Buddy.' Tried teaching the Millies to burp again but they are still rubbish at it. They never go to the toilet either. How weird!

My Superman was ace today but Mum and Father still hate me biking.

Everyone is going mental about the curse but nobody will talk about it.

I must tell mother that her polyester trousers do not suit her bum. She says they are 'slacks.' Who cares! They still look daft.

There is a mole on the close and Father is planning to murder it. I must ask Mr. Sheepsbottom to adopt it.

P.S. I am worried about Mr. Sheepsbottom. He is still glowing pink and doesn't know it. His breakfast is not the reason. He eats cornflakes and not Ready Brek. It doesn't seem right for a very old man. Alex says that it is probably just his 'auwa' whatever that is. I took another photo of it today to show Alex.

P.P.S. Mr. Ramsbottom says he does not mind me calling him Mr. Sheepsbottom, but not in front of the Greygoyles in case it gets me into trouble."

Tiggy was in the attic on an errand rustling up items for a Residents and Villagers Association jumble sale. Her mother was Head of Fundraising for all approved good causes. The first to tickle their fancies was a pet cemetery for R.A.V.A. pets and would be exclusive. However, the Luvvies parrot and any potential snakes or 'unpleasant looking reptiles' would not be allowed in either dead or alive. They had asked Thomas Tipple, as he put it, 'to job the job' and to plan and plant out the memorial gardens. 'Somewhere beautiful and sacred to celebrate their lives,' read the brief. Alex had found the animal thing highly amusing.

'And will the cemeterwy be open before or after all the moles in the neighbourhood have been slaughtered?' he had enquired.

Tiggy loved the attic, all apart from its musty, oniony smell. It was a place of dark corners and eerie shadows. Thick-legged spiders spun silver cobwebs, casting their magic from beam to beam with an atmosphere of intrigue and excitement to set Tiggy's heart racing. It was a treasure trove of surprises and hidden secrets, full of curiosities from a deeply mysterious past that her parents had never wanted to discuss. There were boxes overflowing with photographs, bric-a-brac and toys, a brass horn that had lost its shine and an old-fashioned sewing machine. Everything wore a coat of dust undisturbed for years. It was a time capsule of memories from an unfamiliar time when in Tiggy's mind, dinosaurs probably roamed the Earth and her parents were small children.

In a dusky corner slumped upon a rocking chair a one-eyed doll smiled at her, its glass eye seeming to follow Tiggy's every move. It gave Tiggy the creeps. She picked up a book to take her mind off it, blew away the dust and began turning its yellowed pages. The book had a mysterious charm such as only age can bring and Tiggy was fascinated by the glimpse of days gone by that it gave her:

"One of the cheapest things," she read out loud "is car-cleaning cotton which is bought in bundles of 4 yards. It is a cream knitted soft stretchy material made in the form of a tube. One yard will make a long, roomy beach bag which can also be used at home for storing shoes or knitting, or stockings and gloves."

'What anoraks! Even the Greygoyles aren't this dull!' she muttered admiring a beautifully hand-written message in copperplate script on the inside cover:

"To Georgina Alison

Happy 8th birthday,

Love from Great Aunt Beatrice xxx"

A pressed, four-leafed clover floated out from the book's pages. It had become so transparently thin and faded with the passage of time that it was hard to believe that it could ever have once been alive.

'This 'ud be good for The Stig Man. He could do with some better luck. He's a proud American and wants to go home,' she said glancing at the doll to see if it was still staring at her.

In another cobwebby corner of the attic stood an old dressmaker's dummy wearing a child's shirt and a balding velvet waistcoat. A cotton thread from a missing button dangled from one of the cuffs. The remaining buttons were mother of pearl like the one she had found days earlier in the woods. The waistcoat's velvet, although worn, was still so invitingly soft that Tiggy could not resist trying it on.

'Awh! It drowns me!' she said taking it off again. 'The Stig Man might like it though,' she mumbled hiding it in an old satchel, forgetting that the dressmakers dummy was behind her.

It toppled over, activating an old toy jack-in-the-box whose clown sprang up from its dusty box with one horrendous squawk.

'Watch it creep or you're for the jumble!' said Tiggy almost jumping out of her skin and seeing its jolly face. 'And you!' she snarled having turned and seen the one-eyed doll grinning at her.

Two hours later, she had sorted through much of the family history but she was still no wiser about it.

'How boring!' she said gathering up her father's actuarial study notes that were scattered over a large section of the floorboards.

An old sepia-toned photograph fell out from between some of the sheets. It was of a child dressed in a baggy shirt and breeches, peering beneath the brim of a straw boater and clutching a cuddly toy panda.

'George, aged 7 years,' she read, 'Kinda cute panda!'

she mumbled stuffing the photo into her pocket to show Pants.

A few bagged-up memories later, Tiggy had the jumble sorted ready and waiting by the front door. Surprisingly, her mother, with her artist's pencil still in her hand, was already home from her art class. She had not been gone long and appeared most agitated. Something had definitely happened and Alex and Penelope were trying hard not to laugh.

'Not a stitch on! The man was a complete exhibitionist!' said Alison Tipple blushing and stabbing the air with her pencil. 'How is that 'life drawing?' It has nothing to do with life, either my life or anybody else's! Who goes around naked like that? It's ridiculous!' complained the woman. 'Besides I kept being questioned about Mr. Dodds and Cherie. Just because I got my cleaning stuff off him and Cherie's sister cuts our hair, it does not make me an expert on some wretched curse that has been a thing in this village since before I was even born. It's madness!' she said, doing a full-on flounce through the hall and adjusting the figurine on the hall table. She still felt guilty about Cherie.

Later that evening, Arthur Ramsbottom was in his garden refilling his bird feeder with nuts. A robin was puffing out its feathers and following his every move, pecking at the peanuts he had carelessly let sprinkle onto the ground. Spotting his little neighbour over the hedge, Arthur Ramsbottom beckoned her to join him. Tiggy once again noticed the strange glow surrounding his body and she was determined to photograph it this time in the daylight.

'Evening Miss Tigs! I have something extra special to show you,' said the kindly man, leading her to the far corner of his garden.

It was a shady spot of immense natural beauty. There were toadstool encrusted log piles bolstered with cushions of velvety moss, lush ferns and wild flowers. In the nearby bog garden, a dragonfly swooped above the hostas.

'Did you see that?' asked Tiggy watching as the insect's shimmering wings propelled it in reverse over the bog garden.

It reminded her of the one that had led her to the maze's 'Green Man,' at the heart of The Green Realm.

'It's an Emperor!' said Arthur. 'You can tell by the green body.'

The dragonfly zipped about, going in all directions until it swooped down and settled on Tiggy's shoulder.

'You're going to be lucky!' he added, 'that green dragonfly is an omen.'

The hostas were in a sorry state, their large leaves shredded and full of holes, a sure sign that slugs had feasted upon them. Arthur delicately poked his stick to lift up some fern fronds that were hiding a log-house made from half a barrel.

'A mother hedgehog and her babies are in there,' whispered Arthur beaming like a proud parent.

The sun was sinking like a falling orange and as the two neighbours chatted, sat upon a log, they kept watch over the little house.

'Why were you out in the storm the other night?' Tiggy asked, 'I saw you from my window.'

She stared at her neighbour's rosy glow wondering whether she dared to touch. For once, Arthur Ramsbottom seemed lost for words.

'Let's just say it's brotherly love,' responded Arthur after some careful thought.

'I wouldn't do that for my brother,' said Tiggy noticing that the warm glow surrounding her friend had intensified.

'Ahh but it's cos you still have one,' he replied, his gaze lingering on the bloodshot sky.

At that moment, the mother hedgehog poked her nose outside the house and Arthur hobbled indoors to fetch a saucer of water. Tiggy snapped away with her camera and got the photograph she had so wanted.

Chapter 21

MOLE ON THE LOOSE!

Fresh molehills had sprung up overnight and not a single culprit caught. The mood at Pearly Gates was grim and Alex's glib enquiry, 'Has anybody died?' only served to make matters worse.

'Died! Died!' raged his father thumping his fist on the kitchen worktop and soon regretting it. 'That is just the point...not one of the wretched pests...I am sure those traps were set,' said a bewildered Thomas Tipple scratching his head.

'So you thought that you'd jobbed that job?' Alex asked, shifting from sarcasm to concern.

'Absolutely! I thought I really had well and truly jobbed that job!' his father replied rubbing his hand better.

The truth was simple; there had been no moles caught because no traps had remained set overnight. Tiggy, needing to conceal a guilty conscience, made a hasty exit and a minute later had whistled her way out of the close leaving behind her diary and the truth.

Friday 20th August

"If Father jobs the job and murders the mole, he will not go to heaven. I will pull up the traps and save them both. He thinks he can tame nature but he can't. Nobody can.

P.S. I am having nightmares about The Indigo. I just do not know what to do."

It was 'Stupid O'clock' early and as usual on a Saturday morning, the Gotobeds were out with their dog. They were such creatures of habit that Arthur Ramsbottom had been known to reset his watch according to the time that the trio had passed by his patio windows. The word on the close was that 'Darling' was not responding well to the therapy and that the Gotobeds were wasting their money. The poodle was now wearing pretty transfers on its shaved legs instead of the bracelets, but still insisted upon wearing Emily Gotobed's highly prized emerald and diamond choker as a collar.

When Tiggy arrived at the windmill, the little girl,

complete with straw hat, was by the puddle again. However, her excitement at seeing Millie B instantly evaporated because she was crying. Millie B was making daisy chains, trying to hide her tears as she threaded each stalk to the next.

'S-s-s-sorry!' the girl wailed with a stammering sob throwing the daisy chain into the puddle.

It was just a string of daisies but to Tiggy it was so much more than that. She could feel her friend's pain in every stem and petal. It was a reminder of the daisy her mother had discarded, crushing both her daughter and the flower when she had read her school report, and because she was different. She could feel her friend's sadness and wanting somehow to make things better, she splashed into the puddle to retrieve it. Water drenched her skin and instantly the puddle's wondrous power began to work again. Tiggy was on her way to The Blue Realm.

Meanwhile back at the close, Alicia Duncan Forbes was on the Pearly Gates doorstep paying an unexpected visit. The topiary cockerel, now minus its comb, was looking so dishevelled that Alison Tipple, hoping desperately that her visitor would not notice, tried to stand in front of it. Alicia Duncan Forbes, however, had other things on her mind. The previous day her husband had bought her two more extravagant pieces of jewellery and she was eager to show them to everyone.

'My Rupert says we can't take it with us so we might as well spend it. Look at what happened to Mr. Dodds and that twin,' she said with a smirk, 'Both gone in a flash! He for one, never even owned a decent wristwatch! That's why hubby splashed the cash for me again,' gloated Alicia Duncan Forbes drawing attention to a new sparkling pair of earrings and matching necklace. 'I thought why not invite our ladies to a night of pampering, posh knickers and nibbles,' she said, removing an envelope from her designer handbag. 'Mrs. Gotobed excluded because I'm sure she wouldn't want to leave that silly dog of theirs at home until it has been cured from wearing her jewellery. In my opinion the woman has become quite unhinged about it,' she said trying to force back a grin.

'Both Darling and her jewellery mean so much to her so it's bound to make her stressed,' said Alison Tipple a little concerned that Alicia Duncan Forbes was publicly excluding the woman.

'It's ridiculous when her jewellery is so cheap and, dare I say it, trashy!' hissed Alicia Duncan Forbes smirking at the corners of her lipstick and handing Alison the invitation. 'Seven thirty for eight...come as you are!' brayed the woman, eyeing Alison Tipple's outfit from top to bottom. 'Well perhaps not,' she added noticing the trousers. 'All exclusive ranges and there will certainly be no tacky stuff. We will leave that to the weird goings on of Nightingale Road; and they call them 'Tupperware parties!' Another flash of her new jewels and the dreadful woman was gone.

Alison Tipple watched her from the living room window and took a deep breath.

'Bitches!' she murmured, spotting Darling and Alicia Duncan Forbes in danger of a head-on encounter.

The Gotobeds had just completed their umpteenth circuit of the close when Alicia Duncan Forbes, not wanting to acknowledge the threesome, began rummaging in her bag. It was a manoeuvre too much to ask of her uncoordinated feet. Alicia Duncan Forbes tripped on the kerb and fell flat on her face. She lay on the ground clutching her ankle and crying out in pain, although somehow she managed to keep hold of her new diamonds.

'Go to her, Paul!' ordered Emily Gotobed to her long-suffering husband, a man even more scared by his wife's shadow than he was of his own.

'Go to her,' he repeated out loud obeying the instruction, and dropping his wife's handbag on the ground.

Unfortunately, Darling got there first and squatted to do its business like a mini-Niagara Falls over Alicia Duncan Forbes' new shoes. It was to the secret delight of the Gotobeds, who had not believed that their beloved Darling could possibly act so like a dog.

Perhaps the therapy was working after all.

At lunchtime, Tiggy returned to the close, her eyes shining with the happiness that she felt in her heart. She had ventured into The Blue Realm of the rainbow, and having succeeded in its challenge had added another crystal to her collection. She couldn't help but smile thinking about her time with The Stig Man, and she hoped desperately that her four-leafed clover would bring him the good fortune that he deserved. Tiggy snatched a few more leaves from the topiary cockerel on her way to park her bike and, having checked on Sluggy and Huggy, she breathed a sigh of relief on finding them safe behind the shed.

Tiggy's bedroom was her sanctuary where she hid her rainbow crystals and thought stuff through. She reflected on her rainbow escapades and tried to visualise what dastardly dangerous deed The Indigo would have in store for her. She had found that writing it down had helped ease the burden of keeping The Sacred Secret to herself. It was almost as if by sharing it on paper she was confiding in a friend. Tiggy took her favourite green biro and made a diary note.

Saturday 21st August

'The punk angel is now so hairy he has a bushy beard and dreadlocks. The Stig Man is getting stressy about it. I must take him father's little 'Stay calm to win' book.' He says he is

thinking about going to The Indigo with me. I will try to get a 'pinky promise.' Mrs. D.F's beauty spot = six hairs. She fell flat on her face today. Good! *Personal best record."*

Tiggy emptied her pouch removing her collection of crystals. There were now five of them, each from a different rainbow realm. She showed them all to Pants keeping her newest stone in the palm of her hand. She stared at it thinking about her time with The Stig Man in The Blue Realm and lost herself daydreaming in its icy blue sparkles. However, the sound of Alex singing 'Starman' in the bathroom next door snapped her out of it. He never closed the door for a 'number one' because he said the new avocado suite made him feel 'claustwophobic.' Hearing her brother so close to her secret haul, Tiggy hid the stones beneath her pyjamas because Alex always paid her room a visit after every bathroom trip.

'Didn't know you were interwested in cwystals,' said Alex spotting the book on the bed.

'I'm not particularly. I just got it to please Mum.' Tiggy replied throwing herself down onto her pyjamas as if she was about to score a rugby 'try'.

'Knowledge is power Tig! Never forget it!' said Alex walking away and bursting out into another chorus of the song.

Alex was right. He was always right. She knew

nothing about the crystals that she had worked so hard to earn. Hers were certainly all very different to The Stig Man's, so presumably they must have different powers for different jobs. She knew that he had told her repeatedly that she must never leave home without them. Using her library book, 'Crystal Magic,' for reference she began matching the stones to the pictures and descriptions and reading about their special powers and making a list. Would perhaps sodalite, purple aventurine, lepidolite or dark obsidian and tourmaline be the stone she would find in The Indigo? She stared at the picture and read about the stones' special powers.

'Listen to this bit Pants! Purple aventurine helps you live as your true self. Perfect! It's like we're living in 'Fake Town' with all The Greygoyles and Mum and Father trying so hard to please them.' She read on a bit further, 'and seems like sodalite would heal mum from her awful stammer. That would make her happy.'

Tiggy was beginning to take her role as a 'Rainbow Child' very seriously.

'Knowledge is power!' Tiggy mumbled to Pants as she dozed off on top of her bed with the book still in her hand. It was not long before she was dreaming.

When Tiggy woke up, she had revisited her most recent rainbow adventure in the Blue Realm. She didn't know exactly what it meant because like so many dreams it was a rather insane mash up of what had actually happened with lots of crazy, imagined bits thrown in for good measure. She tried to recall it as best as she could, some bits coming back to her in vivid detail: she had had so much fun swimming with dolphins, bathing beneath a waterfall and catching clouds out of powder blue skies with The Stig Man. However, after The Book of the Realms appeared in her dream, pulsating and glowing blue, The Stig Man had gone and she was fast asleep in a bluebell wood. The colours were glorious and all was peaceful as a flock of bluebirds dropped hundreds of pale blue feathers over her until eventually, she was completely covered and woke up. Tiggy removed her 'Meaning of Dreams' book off her shelf.

'To dream about a bluebird symbolises both happiness and sadness. It is also an indication of purification and resolution in opposing conflicts in your life,' she read aloud. 'Absolutely no idea what that means,' she said to Pants as if the bear might possibly have the answer. 'And blue feathers are a reminder to LISTEN and to accept what others are telling you.' 'Ok! That's easy enough to understand!' she said feeling that it was not quite such a waste of time after all.

Tiggy thought about the rest of her dream. Alicia Duncan Forbes was there trying to steal The Blue Realm's sapphires. She was being so greedy stuffing her pockets and even her colossal shoes full of them until she couldn't possibly carry any more. Suddenly a beady-eyed blue jay had swooped in pecking her to pieces until she surrendered both the sapphires and her diamond ring (the one she called 'her rock') to the bird. Tiggy was again looking through her dream dictionary to make some kind of sense of it all.

'Blue jays in dreams are symbolic of taking action in the direction of the highest truth. The jay asks for honesty and forthrightness. To see birds in your dream symbolises your goals, aspirations and hopes. They are a reminder of happiness and joy that is to come and are about setting yourself free.'

She thought about the last bit of her dream and knew that the appearance of the jay had been an actual replay of what had happened in The Blue Realm and that before parting, The Stig Man had given her a pale blue forget-me-not. Flower or no flower, how could she ever forget her American friend, The Stig Man?

Chapter 22

THE TEA LEAVES

Alison Tipple was counting money from the R.A.V.A's jumble sale and as she added the final one pence coin to the pile, she sighed so deeply that it went all the way down to her fluffy slippers.

'£7.23 what a pittance for the grief it has caused!' said Alison Tipple sighing again.

She was still uneasy that she had sold so many of their old memories and put their past on display. Pearly Gates was not a happy house. Tiggy had taken the opportunity to go back to the mill and hang out with Millie A, even though he was still as shy as ever. The mood at Pearly Gates had changed from bad to worse and the mole was still on the loose creating havoc in the garden. It was all that Thomas Tipple could think about.

'According to the statistics I should have caught that wretched mole three times already by now!' moaned a bad-tempered Thomas Tipple. 'I'll just have to go on mole watch at dawn every day before work.'

Alison Tipple shrugged her shoulders, not really listening.

'And if that fails, I'll jolly well stay up all night at the weekend. That way I can spot the molehills as they come up and catch the menace there and then. I'll get the job jobbed even if it's the last thing I do!' he said checking that the light in his torch was working.

The distraction caused by the moles had been the perfect cover for Tiggy to do what she needed to do. In fact, a few hours later when Tiggy returned with a garland of violets in her hair and a sparkling chunk of amethyst that she had won in The Violet Realm nobody even realised that she had been missing. Everything about the Tipple household was strange as if the carnage of the moles had brought with it its very own black cloud. Thomas Tipple was so absorbed in waging his war against nature that he had not noticed his wife's erratic behaviour. She had shrugged off the ugly black mood of recent days, but had started to behave so unpredictably that it was scary. For two days Alison Tipple had not drawn the living room curtains, the porcelain figurine had been off its spot on the hall table for the entire day, she had poured milk down the toilet and put bleach in the fridge. She had even hung her underwear out in daylight at the risk of the neighbours seeing it. Little things, but they spoke volumes. The children knew that something wasn't right. They lay low, staying in their rooms and Tiggy did not dare to venture out on her bicycle even though she was desperate to return to the mill. Then, as luck would have it, Thomas Tipple had a box of vegetables, straight out of his garden, for Mrs.D and somebody had to take it. Tiggy was more than happy to oblige.

The outside of Mrs.D's house had certainly seen better days, whilst inside the furniture was old-fashioned and worn. Nevertheless, it had such a warm, cosy atmosphere that anybody who sunk into the comfortable chairs, instantly felt at home and wouldn't want to leave. Mrs.D was a champion listener, full of worldly wisdom. She was 'with it,' 'down with the kids,' and was no more offended by punk rockers than she had been of Elvis Presley's gyrating hips. Besides which she would always keep the tea and cakes coming. Mrs.D was simply the salt of the earth, what Alex described as a 'twue bwick'.

The widow ushered her young guest into the 'snug' and then set to work in the kitchen. The 'snug' was what Mrs. Derbyshire called her living room. She seemed to have a magical name for everything. As usual the smell of freshly baked bread filled the house, so unlike Pearly

Gates which always reeked of polish and bleach. It was the difference between a show house and a home. An old grandfather clock ticked loudly in the corner of the room and beneath the window was a threadbare couch buried under a collection of cushions and teddy bears. In one corner of the room stood Mrs. D's sheepskin lined 'cosy boot.' Tiggy had heard all about it, Mrs. Derbyshire having bought it from the market the previous winter had not suffered with a single chilblain ever since. The notion of two feet zipped into one boot had always sounded like a recipe for disaster. It had bothered Tiggy a great deal; in fact, so much so she had even dreamt of the ageing and rotund Mrs.D jumping around the house like a pregnant kangaroo and slipping on a banana skin. Seeing the boot stood there with its fleecy pom poms it looked so harmless. Tiggy was glad about that and decided that she need not worry any more.

The walls of the 'snug' were covered in photographs and 'Mrs. D's Charlie, her much loved, much missed late husband was on every one of them. The biggest, hanging in pride of place above the fireplace was one of Tiggy, sat upon his lap and as she circled the room to look at them all a feast of fond memories came flooding back. On the sideboard was an open scrapbook full of newspaper cuttings from the local press, including those of the latest curse victims and the recent Fun Day. Mrs.

Derbyshire had been in the process of securing them in place when her visitor had unexpectedly arrived. A black and white print of Penelope, radiant in all her princess regalia smiled up at her and turning the page, another of Alicia Duncan Forbes attacking the Mad Maxeman with her handbag made Tiggy chuckle once more. A glorious smell of baking was wafting through from the kitchen and hearing the sound of plates being rattled Tiggy knew that she was in for a treat. The farmer's widow always had a fresh batch of butterfly buns and fairy cakes at the ready in case her little friends called by. No visit was ever inconvenient and nothing was too much trouble. Tiggy continued turning back time with every page of the scrapbook as the cuttings got older and more yellowed. There was even a picture of Timothy Grimshaw with a full head of hair, and yet everybody knew that, in his wife's words, the poor man had been 'follicly challenged' ever since sliced bread had been invented. More and more pictures of past local events sparked distant memories until one final cutting sent an icy chill down her spine as her eyes devoured the headline:

Village Shock As Boy Goes Missing In Storm.

'On the eve of their 10th birthday twins Arthur and Arnold Ramsbottom of Great Snubington, walking the family's pet dog, became victims of a violent storm, that struck the village yesterday evening in an unprecedented wave of destruction. Lightning struck the two boys, who had taken shelter beneath an oak tree on local farmland. The landowner, Edward Derbyshire, aged 51, alerted by the boys Labrador barking outside his farmhouse, discovered Arthur, a member of the local Boys Brigade, trapped beneath a fallen branch. The boy is now in St. Michael's General Hospital, where he remains in a critical condition. Arnold Ramsbottom remains missing and late last night, Chief Inspector Roger Harrington of the local constabulary confirmed that the search for the boy would continue. Mr. Edward Derbyshire, a farmer who, with his 21-year-old son Charles, assisted the rescue teams at the scene, was yesterday too upset to comment.'

The cogs were turning in Tiggy's brain and she was still staring at the pictures of the two brothers and another of the burnt oak tree when the kettle whistled and moments later Mrs. Derbyshire shuffled into the room with a tea tray and a plateful of home-baked treats. Tiggy sunk into the big armchair and began tucking into one of her favourite iced fairy cakes.

'Made from real fairy dust!' said Mrs. Derbyshire.

Tiggy smiled and nodded knowingly, having heard it many times before. The R.A.V.A's jumble sale and a bitchy dispute over a pair of psychedelic designer platform shoes had been the talk of the village and Mrs. Derbyshire wanted the latest gossip.

'The cheek of it!' the old lady said shaking her head, having heard how a stranger to the village had put Alison Tipple under pressure to accept twenty books of 'Green Shield Stamps' instead of cash for a new tape recorder, still in its box, 'Your dear, poor Mummy! She would hate that!'

The Olympic Games and Nadia Comaneci's perfect 10.00s, Alex Tipple's latest almanac predictions and the Pearly Gates mole had all been topics for discussion and Tiggy's humorous interpretation.

'Alex says we'll have moved and got a puppy by Christmas. I reckon there's more chance that Mrs. Duncan Forbes will give Mrs. Gotobed all her jewellery!' laughed the little girl, cradling her tea.

She only liked Mrs.D's tea and always drank squash at home. Mrs. D was convinced that it was because she still used traditional tea leaves, refusing to swap them for the new-fangled tea bags that seemed to be the rage.

'It will take more than a cheeky chimp on a telly advert to persuade me to switch to bags! You just can't beat tea leaves in a china cup for a tasty brew,' Mrs.D would chuckle.

She was a wiz at what Tiggy called 'cosy caring.' She felt at home and sipped her tea very slowly because she wanted to stay longer. Not that Mrs.D would have minded if she had stayed there all day. Tiggy took her final sip but still not ready to leave, she passed the china cup to her elderly friend.

'Go on then,' said Tiggy with an impossible to refuse smile.

It was common knowledge in the village that the widow could foresee a person's future by reading the tea leaves left in the bottom of their cup. She had predicted only weeks earlier that there would be two more curse victims. Alicia Duncan Forbes had accused her of being 'a witch' and was petitioning to have her removed from the village. Mrs. Derbyshire hesitated. She had never read them for a child before but she didn't want to disappoint her visitor.

'Please!' Tiggy said passing Mrs.D her cup. 'Love you forever!' she pleaded pushing the cup into her hand with a glinty grin.

Mrs. Derbyshire would have found saying 'no' to Tiggy almost as hard as having to burn all her dear husband's photographs. She smiled and taking her time, studied the clusters of tea leaves stuck to the bottom of the cup. Mrs.D's face was serious, her brow furrowed, looking nothing like her usual jolly light heartedness. Then eventually she cleared her throat to speak.

'I see a new friendship, Tiggy,' she said looking deep into her eyes. 'It's someone you can trust. I can see that they're a good sort! That's nice!'

The old lady smiled and patted Tiggy on her knee before looking into the cup again.

'I can see you having so much fun my lovely...there's so many bright colours,' she said looking happy.

Mrs. Derbyshire returned her focus to the cup searching for more meanings and omens but after a few seconds, her smile faded and then there was a long delay until she frowned,

'There's trouble at home dear...your mummy and daddy aren't happy,' she said with a sigh.

'That will be the mole,' Tiggy nodded in agreement, 'It's been going mental!'

Mrs. Derbyshire shook her head. 'It seems more than that...there is sadness.'

The old lady studied more closely a group of tea leaves stuck to the back of the cup. Suddenly her face darkened and the smile wiped clean from her lips. She stared and stared into the cup saying nothing for two long minutes as if she was hoping and waiting for something to change.

'The arch stayed partly blurred,' Mrs. Derbyshire said as she tipped the tea leaves first one way and then the other before returning the cup to its saucer. 'A disastrous journey!' she mumbled 'It just wouldn't completely clear!'

'Go on Mrs. D ....Please say more!' urged Tiggy.

The kindly old lady took the little girl's hands and looked at her in such a way that Tiggy could feel not only her love, but her anxiety too.

'There's danger Tiggy. I saw ants. You have something difficult ahead. I want you to be careful,' she said. 'I saw it...there in the cup. A cup full of pretty colours that turned black. There are dark forces at work, Tiggy, that you must not disturb. There were tears falling like rain....'

Still holding the child's hands, the widow drew herself in even closer and stared into the little girl's eyes.

'Promise me you'll be careful and not do anything silly.'

Tiggy could feel Mrs. Derbyshire's breath upon her skin.

When the clock chimed twelve, Tiggy left with her usual parting gift of a dip dab, a tube of hard-boiled Spangles and a paper bag of Black Jacks and Fruit Salad chews. Then as sure as night follows day, they rounded off their visit with the most bearsome of hugs.

'Remember what I said now!' shouted the old lady as her young friend cycled away across the yard.

Tiggys's head felt so full, as if it could burst with a million thoughts that she did not notice when Pants was catapulted from her rucksack. She thought about Mrs. Derbyshire's warning and considered what the difficult journey and the danger could mean.

'It has to be The Indigo. It just has to be!' Tiggy mumbled. 'What am I to do?' she said, looking up to the sky.

Tiggy felt torn. She had promised The Stig Man she would return but leaving her family when the stakes were so high risk seemed selfish and wrong. What if she failed like The Stig Man and never made it back? Tiggy stared into the blueness as if expecting the answer to be there. Should she forget about the one remaining rainbow realm? Both Mrs.D and the tea leaves seemed to be telling her that she should. However, Tiggy did not like the thought of always asking herself 'What if…?' She knew that never having the answers to this question would torment her. Arthur Ramsbottom had told her that a 'What if' was a monster that strangled lives.

She cycled on weighing up her options and their pros and cons, her mind wavering like a candle in the wind. She could hear Alex even though he wasn't there.

'You're stuck between a wock and a hard place, Tig! You can't win!'

That of course was not much help. It purely reinforced her dilemma.

'What would Mr. Ramsbottom do?' Tiggy muttered to herself. She looked up to the sky once more and it gave her the answer she had been searching for by day and by night.

'Go with your heart! It's the only voice you will ever regret not listening to.'

Mr. Ramsbottom's words kept repeating in her head.

All she had to do now was to work out what her heart was telling her. She put a hand to her chest, hoping to feel her heartbeat, hoping to feel the answer. Tiggy's head was still spinning as she approached the lightning tree. She paused a moment to ponder the newspaper story in Mrs. Derbyshire's scrapbook. She stared at the pale silvery branches, so stark in their nakedness,

'Poor Mr. Sheepsbottom! I know now why your leg is wonky,' she sighed before riding on.

The drone of lawnmowers and the smell of freshly mown grass welcomed Tiggy back to Heavenly Gardens. Pearly Gates now had a skip in its driveway but everything else was the same: Harry 'Flash' Dobson was polishing his brass knocker and The Riches' children because of the Residents ban on ball games, were using a cleverly tied rolled up pullover as a football instead.

'Some things never change,' mumbled Tiggy to herself but soon she would discover just how wrong she could be.

Chapter 23

SECRETS
AND SURPRISES

'I'm a man on a mission!' Thomas Tipple declared. 'I'll job that job even if it kills me!'

He was holding a box containing five new mole traps.

'Once these beauties are in place it'll put pay to the pest!' he muttered.

The mole was living on borrowed time and so, too, was any other living thing that threatened his garden. Nature really could be such a pain.

It was game over too for Sluggy and Huggy. The slugs had done well to survive for so long but it didn't make it any easier for Tiggy. Death was death. It was so final.

'Fancy drowning in beer!' she said looking at the dead slugs floating in the jam jar.

For the first time her bike did not seem to be important and propping it up against the skip, she began to prepare their graves.

Alison Tipple had been having a major clear out. The R.A.V.A's jumble sale had seemed to have affected her and she had been an emotional wreck ever since. Nobody knew why exactly and nobody dared to ask. All the second-hand furniture given to the Tipples to start their married life now sat in the skip. This included the bed that Alison Tipple had had as a child and even her baby 'blankie' was on the scrap heap. There had not been the least hint of sentimentality about parting with any of it. Alison Tipple had in fact, remarked that she was 'glad to be shot of it all.'

Later that same day, the slugs' funeral had gone off fine. Alex had pitched in with a eulogy for his sister's 'chewished Awian distinctus,' and had done the 'Ashes to ashes, dust to dust' bit lowering the matchbox coffins into the dug-out graves behind the potting shed where the slugs had lived. Finally, a cross, made from lollipop sticks marked their final resting place whilst daisies and buttercups threaded together made a delicate wreath. Apart from Alex, Tiggy had been the only mourner and had wept for them as the pets that they had been to her.

Fair to say, the funeral had thrown a bit of a curve

ball to her normal routine. It was early evening when Tiggy remembered that she still needed to put away her bike. She rounded the corner of the house to one of her worst possible nightmares. Both the skip and her bike had gone! Tiggy could not believe her eyes and screaming like a banshee she woke Dartanian, the Grimshaws' guard dog several doors up the close.

'No! Please tell me it's a bad dream!' she wailed and for a girl who seldom cried she found herself wiping away her tears for the second time that day.

What a brute of a day it had been! There had been ominous warnings, bereavement and loss of things that she most cherished and when at bedtime she discovered that Pants too was missing the tragedy was complete. Tiggy could not sleep, constantly mulling over the horror story of her last 24 hours. Her whole life had been completely de-railed. The Indigo, too, would be mission impossible without a bike, but she could not breathe a word of her inner turmoil and the decisions that she must make.

The house was hushed apart from Tiggy's heart-rending sobs. The bedroom door creaked open and Tiggy, expecting it to be either Penelope or Alex, could not have been more surprised when her mother sat down on the side of her bed. Alison Tipple, with her back to the weeping child, began speaking more candidly than ever before.

'Pants was mine you know...the best Christmas present that I ever had,' said Alison Tipple, her eyes searching and her head buzzing, undecided as to whether she should turn the key that would open the door to her past. She had not been in this room for years. Her daughter sobbed again, and that settled it.

'He was the only soft toy I ever had,' said Alison Tipple keeping her back to her daughter.

'Both of us were mistakes and I was the biggest because my father wanted a boy. I was such a disappointment.'

She had a lump in her throat and paused to keep her emotions in check before continuing.

'Looking back, I suppose that's why he called me George. I hated it! 'George Applegate,' he used to say, 'you should have been a boy! A man needs a son!'

She paused to reflect, turning back the clock and delving further into the blacked out recesses in her mind. It was true. Her whole existence had been one huge error. Alison Tipple was the unwanted product of a drunken night out and worse still, was a 'she' and not a 'he.' Her entire childhood she had so desperately wanted to be wanted. She had felt her worthlessness in every bone of her body, wearing it like a suit of shame beneath her boyish clothes. Alison Tipple composed herself and took a few more steps down memory lane.

'That's why when Father and I got married I

decided to make a fresh start and use my middle name. I never really liked the name Alison, but as 'George,' I had never been happy. My father blamed me for his drinking and for us being poor. Sometimes regretting it the next day, he used to teach me to wrestle. He would even call me 'Miss George' to let me know that he was sorry. I could always smell the drink on his breath,' Alison Tipple shuddered, pausing once again. 'But my mother still called me Georgina or sometimes Georgie when she was happy...I liked that,' she said, her small voice shrinking even more. 'But that wasn't often. My father was a drinker - a shirker, not a worker. Day and night, he would be in the pub spending what little we had and ending up angry about it. This one particular Christmas,' Alison Tipple coughed nervously, 'my father had bought a raffle ticket in the pub. Now, either he was too drunk to realise he had the winning ticket or else he didn't care because he had won a cuddly toy. 'Beers' were what mattered to him, not 'bears!' and he staggered home leaving the ticket behind on the bar.' Alison Tipple paused again looking into the dark shadows of the room to her past that she had reluctantly opened. 'But a f...f...few days l...later,' she began to stammer, 'the little b...b...bear turned up on our doorstep with a scribbled note arou...around its neck, 'won in raffle. Tic...tic...ticket 60.' One week later on Christmas m...m...m...morning, the panda turned up on my b...b...bed.' She sighed. 'It was the most ma... magical Christmas ever,' she said sounding very distant. 'I called him 'Mr. Sixty' after the number of the winning ticket. At n...night I'd hug him every time I h...h...heard the shouting and f...fighting downstairs and my mo... mother crying...and then the heavy footsteps c...c... coming up the stairs...and I'd hide under the bedclothes j...just me and Mr. Sixty.'

Alison Tipple paused to reflect again. For the first time she turned to look glassy-eyed at her own little girl, and as Tiggy's heavy lids closed again, she stroked her daughter's hair just once, and then turned off the light.

However, Tiggy did not sleep for long. She fought with her quilt, tossing and turning like dirty laundry in a washing machine. She dreamt darkly of Mr. Sixty, her Pirate Pants, being held hostage in The Indigo Realm and his release hinging on Mikey Mucus forwarding a huge ransom of his rare glow-in-the-dark bogies. It was just one of her many nightmares about The Indigo, and awake or asleep, her fear of the realm was beginning to boss her mind. Tiggy woke with a start, but her instant relief at it all having been a silly dream evaporated, as soon as she reached out for Pants and discovered that her little companion really had gone. The downstairs clock struck three but Tiggy could not wait any longer to find Pants and bring him safely home.

The moon was shining brightly when Tiggy stepped outside. There was a real nip to the air but otherwise it was a perfect night for star-gazers. The sky, like a black canvas sprinkled with silver glitter, twinkled in every direction. Alex had taught her about stars and planets and as she gazed up at her favourite constellation, she etched her finger along the 'w' of Cassiopeia. The only noise was from her own squeaking footsteps as she picked her way across the damp grass towards the garden sheds. Curiously, a light was on in the 'Jobs been jobbed' shed, just as there had been on the night of the storm. Her father had been spending more and more of his time in there over recent days and weeks.

'Father will take root in there if he spends any longer in that shed of his!' his wife had complained.

She had a point. Tiggy sneaked up to the window and crouching down, peeked inside. She could hardly believe her eyes to see her father, a.k.a. 'Corduroy Man' sat at his desk dressed in black leathers and pouring over some pictures in a magazine. Suddenly as if he had sensed that someone was watching him, he stood up and glanced towards the window but his daughter had already bopped down out of sight.

Tiggy had no time for this mystery, she had another one far more important to solve; Pants was out there somewhere and all alone. She sneaked through the gap in the hedge and into the Ramsbottoms' garden.

Only her sunflowers witnessed her enter the next door's shed and come out with the bike belonging to the Ramsbottoms' granddaughter who was still away cruising the world. Tiggy knew that Beverly wouldn't mind.

It was a magical night for cycling to Mrs. Derbyshire's but with Tiggy's heart still aching over the loss of Sluggy and Huggy, and Pants lost in the dark and all alone, her insides felt battered and bruised. Her rainbow crystals, stowed away in her kangaroo top's pouch, and supposedly full of fixing powers, were doing nothing to ease the pain. Beverly's new bike was much bigger than her old one and struggling to reach the pedals made the search more difficult. Tiggy swung her flashlight from side to side but reluctantly she had to admit that even beneath the moonlight and diamond sky it was impossible to look properly for Pants in the dark. Having scanned the cycle path, the ground beneath the Lightning Tree, where she had briefly stopped on her last visit, as well as Mrs. Derbyshire's yard it pained her that there was no sign of the bear. She consoled herself that it would not be long until first light when she would most surely find him.

Just as the day had been one of upsets, the night was to be one of surprises: first her mother's candid confessions and her father dressed in leathers in his shed, then followed by yet another unexpected event that would unfold before her eyes. The mill stood in water and at its edge, The Millies were weeping. Their tears were falling like rain into what had started out as just a puddle but now resembled a moving lake, ebbing and flowing around the mill. Tiggy spied from behind a tree, photographing them, secretly snapping away until she had finished off the film. 'The Millies' continued to cry and the puddle of tears swelled. Millie A and Millie B were her friends, the very same children she had laughed and played with and dreamt about all summer. However, this time she dared not intrude. Their grief seemed so intensely raw and personal, a private matter for sharing only with each other. The children had cried until daybreak and when the dawn chorus burst forth and the sun sprinkled the earth with its golden light, Tiggy watched them walk away and disappear into the hazy purple woods. The whole thing had puzzled her.

'The Millies tears! So that's what it is!' said Tiggy, sat astride her bike. She stared into the lake looking as deeply as she could, 'I really never knew they were so unhappy!'

It seemed odd to her when she thought about the times they had shared; too many happy memories to count. Did their tears have special properties that had transported her to the rainbow and could they explain this summer's unusual events? Tiggy dipped her finger into the cool depths of the lake. She tasted a drop upon her tongue instantly recognising the saltiness. Suddenly as the salt dissolved, an almighty surge like a tornado consumed her and her bike. It was a blast so powerful that it reached as far as the Derbyshires' farmhouse, sweeping Tiggy high into the sky and moments later, she and her bike were gone.

Mrs. Derbyshire who as a farmer's wife had always been an early bird, now as a farmer's widow was still up catching the worm. She was outside in the chicken coop collecting the eggs from her brood. Unexpectedly and inexplicably, an egg was blown clean out of the widows' hands and smashed at her feet on the ground.

Chapter 24

THE DECISION

'Indigo or bust!' shouted The Stig Man, but Tiggy couldn't see him amidst the fog. A sea of mist blinded her in all directions. It smothered her goose pimpled body feeling like cold damp kisses upon her skin. Everything felt foreign and slightly hostile to her, unlike any of the other rainbow realms, but just knowing that her friend was there was instantly a comfort.

'Miss!' called out The Stig Man until the dark outline of his body steered her towards him. He was standing by a large black hole. 'What kept ya Miss Tiggy? I've waited here for days. I'd nearly given up on ya,' said The Stig Man giving her a hug.

Tiggy didn't feel cold anymore; just seeing her friend and the warmth of his greeting had evaporated the cold mist upon her skin. She pulled back the stretchy waistband of his underpants and released it to deal him a stinger. The boy pretended that it hurt and they both laughed.

'How long have you got! It's been a right nightmare!' Tiggy said. 'The oldies have been proper playing up. Father murdered my slugs and then you won't believe it, to top it all, I went and lost Pants and my bike got skipped!'

The boy pulled a face that melted into a grin, his brace glinting as they did 'The Special Buddy' handshake.

She hesitated, 'The truth is I sort of scared myself and lost my nerve,' said Tiggy.

'Understandable! This is the big one, Girlie. The Book of The Realms and your angel never venture there. It's gonna be epic. You sure will soon be at The Rainbow's End and it will be life-changing for ya Miss Tiggy. I wanted to say goodbye.'

Tiggy didn't feel ready for goodbyes, or at least not forever goodbyes. She looked down into the hole, trying not to cry. It was a grimly dark prospect and although she didn't like to admit it, The Stig Man was a boy who had become a very special friend. This was not a crush or silly infatuation, it was so much deeper than that, and Tiggy hated the thought of leaving him behind, perhaps forever.

'Who else can you go crystal jumping or rainbow

dust kicking with?' she asked fighting back the tears.

'Never mind that, Miss. Focus!' said the boy concealing his own sadness. 'You really grafted for those crystals. They have special powers that could change everything. You deserve to live out your biking dreams!'

Tiggy was not convinced that a few pretty stones could be deal breaking, life-changers and a guarantee of a better life. How could she leave her friend behind, perhaps forever? How could any of this ever fix the pain she was feeling? Unable to hold back the tears any longer, they fell freely, The Stig Man gently wiping them away with his dreadlocks.

'Trust me, I'm The Stig Man!' he said 'The goss on the Angel Tree is that a massive Sacred Stone is the doorway into The Rainbow's End. Then as you Brits say, Bob's your uncle!'

'Actually, it's Trevor, Uncle Trevor,' corrected Tiggy looking so serious that the boy couldn't help but smile at his friends literal take on everything he said.

'Come with me! You promised me you'd think about it!' begged Tiggy tugging his arm. 'I'm not going to lie, but I'm scared.'

The Stig Man gazed deep into the sparkling green pools of her eyes and shuddered.

'I've tried hard to behave with respect and do the right things to make up for my big mouth but the rainbow guys won't buy it. That Wobniar dude is still not happy with me. I gave away The Sacred Secret and seems like that was that!' he said his hand swiping from left to right in a decisive motion.

'Angel Gregory Cecil is still missing a halo and hairy, and without an angel's blessing, I'd end up stuck in The Indigo forever on a one-way ticket to hell.' He took hold of Tiggy's trembling hand. 'It's nothing to worry about …a few dopey bats and a stinky swamp. Just remember, fear is a choice. It is only scary if you decide that it is. Trust me!' he said trying to sound confident so that she would be, too. 'You'll be fine!'

Angel Seraphina pressed down warmly upon her shoulder and then caressed her spine, all the way down to her toes, blessing the girl on her way. Tiggy knew that this was it. This was what being a Rainbow Child, a chosen one, was all about. This was her calling, her destiny. She shuddered and stared into the uninviting blackness of the hole and as her feet disappeared into the mist, a haunting peace enveloped the children. It was as if they stood at the edge of the world with only their friendship between them.

'You've got this!' said The Stig Man, 'there are no second chances. Do it for me Miss Tiggy!'

Tiggy looked for the usual cheeky twinkle in his eyes but they had a seriousness that she had never seen before.

'So, is this really the last time?' she asked feeling

like she had swallowed a boulder.

'There's a last time for everything for everyone. Sure, it's just how it is. 'Take this!' he said slipping a cold, chunky lump into her hand, 'it's my crystal from The Blue Realm.'

Tiggy stared at the glitter-flecked chunk of midnight blue and thought how different it was to her own crystal of ice blue aquamarine from the same realm.

'It's a friendship stone and it will protect you from danger,' he said pressing it into her palm.

'I can't take it!' replied Tiggy trying to give the stone back to him. You may need it one day.'

'Ma heart's in America and always will be but this is my home now...It's okay. Make me proud and do it for me...please!' he said biting his quivering bottom lip, covering his own sadness.

'Besides, who knows what will happen now that I've got this!' he said removing the four-leafed clover from his pocket that Tiggy had given him. 'Who knows what good fortune this will bring me.'

The Rainbow Children squeezed hands, The Stig Man secretly dropping the friendship stone into Tiggy's top's kangaroo pouch. They hugged in silence and did 'The Special Buddy,' but this time, the touch lingered, not wanting to let go.

Tiggy neither said 'goodbye' nor did she look at her friend or she would never have taken the drop. She took one small step, and like a marine diver plunging into the ocean, her trembling body disappeared into the mysterious time-warp depths. The Indigo's force was dragging her down into the darkness and yet vivid flashbacks of her Rainbow Quest played out clearly into her consciousness. The Yellow Realm's frightened Elfibub, the peace loving Greengrungers in The Green Realm, images from The Book of The Realms and her many escapades with The Stig Man all flashed before her. It was like a movie of best memories until she reached The Indigo Realm, the rainbow's underworld.

Chapter 25

THE INDIGO

The Indigo Realm was no place for a child. A god-forsaken pit of inky light, pungent smells and ghastly noises, this was a lost and forbidden world. All the bad and negative energy of the rainbow realms ended up here amidst a steaming swamp from out of which rose the magnificent Sacred Stone. A spectacular monolith of indigo black obsidian, only the Sacred Stone had the power to form a shield against the negative energies of the Indigo Realm. It was its only safe place. If The Red Realm was the rainbow's heart, then The Indigo was its soul but it was a black soul. Nobody or nothing could have prepared Tiggy for this. It was like when you have known for a while that someone you love is about to die and then it happens and you still aren't ready. This was the same, no matter how much The Stig Man had told her or her mind played out the horror tales in her head, it was still that raw first time and the overwhelming power of something that is real and not conjecture. Tiggy was in The Indigo and actually being there was nothing as she expected. Her blood ran cold, trembling and shivering in a state of shock. The Indigo was enough to make anybody scream but it would have been pointless because nobody would have heard her, or at least, not anybody human. The air was thick with dust reeking of death and decay absorbed from the swamp's putrid vapours. Tiggy held her nose, taking long deep breaths but the vile stench overpowered her fight as her stomach retched and heaved. When moments later her jaw set and she had that weird tingling sensation, she knew that she would throw up and seconds later, she could hold it back no longer.

The Indigo was the rainbow's sin bin, a dumping ground for all the rotten energy. It ended up in the swamp that was also home to the Ogi. These were ugly creatures with seven destroyer tentacles, one for each coloured rainbow realm. They defended the Sacred Stone, feeding upon the souls of failed Rainbow Children. The Ogi stripped them bare, destroyed auras and invaded minds to replace anything that was good with what was bad. They condemned these children once back home to see and live life forever in black and white.

The vile stench continued to punish until Tiggy had nothing left to vomit. Gruesome groans, muffled moans and chilling screams echoed. The sound of suffering was everywhere. Tiggy covered her ears but nothing could block out the hideous noise coming from the caves that surrounded The Indigo Realm. These were the Doom Tombs and Tiggy dreaded what she would see. However, as so often happens, especially when you are as nosy as Tiggy, curiosity won the battle with fear and it made her look. Banished Karma Charmas from the realms languished in torture, stripped bare of their positive energy and crystals. They could not move. It had happened when the glow surrounding their bodies had faded out. The banished Karma Charmas wailed as another new arrival shrieked. Faceless spirits with huge skulls and hearts of stone smashed its beating heart to a pulp. Heart breakers and the broken, villains and victims, the vicious and the vulnerable locked together in an eternal hell. Only the bats and beezelfibubs hanging from the caves bore witness. All around the acrid dust of negative energy arrived in black clouds from the rainbow realms. Its bitterness tasted in every breath but the bats and beezelfibubs greedily feasted upon it like a delicacy or favourite meal. They only gave way to the Dreamstealers, the most sinister scavengers of all. Diabolical creatures resembling black feathered angels with huge skulls and black hearts, the

Dreamstealers ruled the highest strata of The Indigo. Their presence was obvious by the chilling sound of slurping as they inflated the sacks upon their back. They were sucking up the energy from stolen dreams, until all hopes were lost and desires shattered. They ruthlessly demolished dreams, broke spirits and moved on. This was a hellhole of fear and destruction, where only what was bad was good and from which a Rainbow Child had disappeared and had never returned. It was the rainbow's underworld where unfortunate souls were a hostage to mercy but there was no mercy...not in The Indigo.

Tiggy trembled, her eyes on stalks screaming as terror shook her bones, living and breathing through every clammy pore. Her life flashed before her as she kept hearing Mrs. D's voice telling her to be careful. She thought about her last visit, that last time. Would it be THE last time? Death felt close and yet never before had she felt so alive. That is how it is when stuff is scary and adrenalin takes charge. It gushed through her veins, her heart pounding as if doing the high jump in her chest. There could be no way out, she was there for a reason. 'Indigo or bust,' was what The Stig Man had said. Angel Seraphina had not even made her presence felt. The Stig Man had been right about that and Tiggy knew that this was her battle, one that she would have to face and fight alone.

If you ignore the rotten stench, the blood curdling sounds and deathly darkness, The Indigo, on paper, was worthy of one of those 'must see before you die destinations.' Here was home to the Sacred Stone, a magnificent smoky, sparkling bulk of indigo black obsidian, towering over the swamp. It was a wonder lost on Tiggy, startled by the ghastly noise overhead of a Dreamstealer. Louder and louder became its foreboding, deathly slurp as the hideous creature moved in, coming closer and closer. The wailing and shrieking from the Doom Tombs deafened. Tiggy covered her ears. She did not know which way to turn or what to do but the magnetism of The Sacred Stone was pulling her by a force too powerful to resist, the swamp remaining the enemy between them. This was a moving sewer of stinking filth made from the raw components of bad impulses including anger, envy, greed and fear. A number of boulders protruded like safe islands, inviting her to jump amidst the dangers of the swamp. Tiggy leapt onto the nearest, the Ogi rearing up their ugly heads. They hissed and flicked out their spear-like tongues that could strike like lightning and were destroyers. Tiggy's legs wobbled but they were biker strong and held firm on the stone. Jumping again onto one safe island after another she threaded her way closer to The Sacred Stone. What she did not know was what she did not know. The Indigo was about to tell her and reveal its terrifying truth.

The Ogidni guarded the Sacred Stone. It was a killer. Sinister and serpent like, it had a thick, tubular body that wrapped itself so tightly around the stone that it was as if it were trying to crush it. It had seven heads, each independent of the other and one for every rainbow realm. It was impossible to tell whether they were awake or asleep until it struck. Then it was too late. It was deadly. Tiggy did not see it first. She could smell it. The Ogidni reeked of every bad smell you can think of: dirty bins, dog poo, cheesy feet, rotten eggs and rotting flesh, and the list goes on. Tiggy retched and her stomach churned like nothing she had ever known, as if her insides were trying to leap outside of her body. It did not seem possible that she could reach The Sacred Stone....not with this.

'Fight!' her fierce inner voice ordered, forcing back her tears.

Tiggy could feel the warmth rising up from the swamp but her whole body was shaking and shivering with shock. She hoped that Angel Seraphina would guide her. Instinct was telling her to turn back although her inner voice told her that the Sacred Stone had to be the way.

'Why leave me, Seraphina, when I need you most?' she whispered hoping that her angel would hear and come back to help her.

Tiggy began to retreat, stepping back across the stones, many with real distance between them. The Ogi were writhing in the swamp, willing her to fall. They wanted to devour her soul.

'You can do it, Tig!' she told herself, getting ready to take another step backwards.

She moved her eyes from stone to feet and back as she spotted her landing. It was almost like being on her bike again but, this time, her cycling skills became survival skills. She took a deep breath, priming herself to leap when a familiar voice cut through the eeriness.

'No! Don't jump, Miss Tiggy!'

'No! Don't jump, Miss Tiggy!' repeated the echo.

It was The Stig Man.

The Stig Man, her trusted friend, was stepping frantically across the stones in a heroic bid to reach her. Suddenly, her chosen 'safe stone' shockingly rose up from behind and out of the depths of the swamp, emerged a grotesque three-legged beast with a single hollow eye towering over her. The terrifying swamp monster roared three times out of its cave-like mouth before slumping down into the swamp again, its eye remaining at the surface, camouflaged like a stone. The Stig Man jumped again and joined his friend upon her island. Whatever good things Tiggy felt being with him again, did not show as they did The Special Buddy without a smile.

'C'mon Miss, we've got this!' he whispered, the age difference between them now seeming much greater than it had before.

Tiggy huddled up close to him but suddenly there was another deafening roar as the beast rose up on its tripod again, its cavernous mouth looking like it could swallow them both.

'Never turn your back on the Sacred Stone,' urged The Stig Man. The 'WhatIf' will get you. A few weeks ago, it swallowed up a dude for quitting their quest and never finding out what might have been. Like any 'what if' in life, it's a killer.'

'C'mon,' he said grabbing her by the arm.

United in friendship and their quest, the two rainbow children jumped together landing closer to The Sacred Stone and the hideous beast disappeared back into the swamp. Moving forward was the only option and holding hands, with every step they gained a little more ground, closing the distance until the elusive Sacred Stone stood before them. All seven heads of The Ogidni appeared to be asleep, as it coiled menacingly around the stone. One final extra-long and tricky leap remained. It demanded greater agility and commanded extra respect such that the children would jump one at a time.

'You go first Miss! I'll follow!' said The Stig Man giving Tiggy one last, gentle and encouraging nudge.

She took her final leap as her friend looked on protectively, but suddenly, the farthest of the Ogidni's heads awoke and viciously lurched towards him. The serpent hissed, firing black missiles of slimy gunk, powerfully hitting The Stig Man in the chest. This would be the killer serpent's only warning. The next would be fatal.

Tiggy had reached The Sacred Stone. Six of the Ogidni's heads were definitely asleep and the other though active and menacing was not near. For a single perfect instant, the wailing from the Doom Tombs stopped. A glorious haze scattered its soft beams upon the swamp and a hidden door in The Sacred Stone slid open. It all happened so quickly, a most beautiful moment in the most unlikely of places, both uplifting and magnetic, drawing Tiggy through and beyond. A beautiful golden light shone forth, warm and soft to the skin and choirs of angels beckoned. Tiggy looked anxiously to The Stig Man, still stranded in the swamp.

'Go!' shouted the boy, 'I'm coming, Miss Tiggy!' he called as he jumped towards her.

'Go! I'm coming, Miss Tiggy!' came the echo.

Tiggy, drawn into the invisible doorway's golden light reached out her arm to her friend. For a second, the children's fingertips tantalisingly touched before the stone door closed between them, leaving The Stig Man behind.

Chapter 26

THE RAINBOW'S END

Angel Seraphina welcomed The Rainbow Child. Her halo of sunflowers was shining brilliantly and as she escorted Tiggy through "The Golden Valley," choirs of angels sang. The darkness had lifted, and just as at sunrise when the world becomes awash with colour and sparkling with dewy newness, there was the same feeling of hope and renewal. Tiggy stared at The Indigo's crystals of purple aventurine, sodalite, lepidolite, black tourmaline and obsidian in her hand and at her skin bathed in a golden light, knowing that she had finally reached The Rainbow's End. Over the past few weeks, she had spent lots of time trying to imagine what it would actually be like. Normally she had settled on the idea of a perfect playground paradise.

'Not what I expected!' she murmured feeling surprised that there were no girls adorned in flowers, skipping with golden ropes or boys racing on silver space hoppers.

Nevertheless, The Rainbow's End was a happy place that both looked and smelt delicious and was gloriously bursting with colour.

'I did it!' she whispered to herself, feeling the relief travel through her body as if somebody was wrapping her in cotton wool.

There was not a child in sight, but it sounded like a schoolyard. Playgrounds the world over sound the same, that excited wall of noise, and this was like that. Small footprints cast in gold dust were everywhere and each time she stepped upon them, a happy child laughed back. The warmth of Angel Seraphina's embrace made her feel cosy and secure now that the turmoil and terrifying trial of The Indigo was over. She was safe and at peace. Her eyes feasted upon candy trees with fruit drop leaves, cream soda fountains that sprayed their sweetness upon her tongue and unicorns of every rainbow colour surrounded a hauntingly beautiful tree. It was very different to any that she had ever seen before. It was like a ballerina, delicate and elegant but with a mighty and invisible strength. Tiggy stared into the tangled mass of twisted, wispy boughs.

'Penelope would love this!' she murmured.

There were faces amongst the ghostly bareness, all of them beautiful and serene. One by one, the branches unravelled. They stripped away like ballet dancers draping swathes of voile until eventually a circle of gently singing angels remained. At its very heart, gleaming and spectacular, was The Pot of Gold.

'So this is The Angel Tree! The Stig Man was right. It is beautiful!' Tiggy mumbled.

The Rainbow Child had been so brave going into The Indigo to help her, knowing without an angel on the other side to greet him, he would never make it there. She wanted more than anything to see his cheeky smile and for him to be standing with her in front of The Angel Tree that he had so often mentioned. For Tiggy, The Stig Man was the only thing missing for things to be perfect because The Rainbow's End was just like paradise in a child's dream.

Suddenly the chorus of angels got louder and reached a crescendo. The Wobniar made his entrance, followed by a flock of bluebirds and robins, and an odd, scaly creature, mostly reptile and yet faintly human that followed behind them. Tiggy thought it was a bit like a giant chameleon gone wrong. The Wobniar's crystal tooth glinted when he smiled, his long hair flashing with every rainbow colour. Seated upon his throne, he raised his crystal sabre and everywhere fell silent, signalling he was about to speak.

'We welcome you, Rainbow Child, at your journey's end. You have been an excellent scholar and have successfully completed your quest. You have respected The Sacred Secret, facing the dilemmas and questions asked of you to overcome its many challenges. As a Rainbow Child, you have put into practice the lessons of The Book of The Realms whilst searching your soul, opening your heart, and energising your mind. You have a gift of colour. It is pure and strong, ready for sharing so that your gift may be theirs. Prepare for The Crystal Ceremony! It is time to bring colour into others' lives and make a lasting change.'

The guarding angels made way for the Guardian of the Rainbow to approach The Pot of Gold for the crystal ceremony to begin. The Wobniar swished his crystal sabre through the air bringing it down onto the golden vessel and immediately it lit up like a huge plasma screen. A series of familiar images appeared that Tiggy was instantly intrigued to watch. The first to appear was her father, dressed from top to toe in leathers. He was in his 'Jobs been jobbed' shed staring at a magazine and looked so shifty that it made her feel uncomfortable in case she should be prying. It was as if her father was hiding a dark forbidden secret that was about to be revealed, but for her mother then suddenly appearing on the screen. Alison Tipple was standing on the Pearly Gates doorstep and Alicia Duncan Forbes was shouting and screaming at her.

'Bully!' Tiggy said under her breath feeling the emotion welling up in her as Alicia Duncan Forbes was wagging her finger and threatening her mother.

Alison Tipple was shrinking inside her clothes, blushing and timid. Tiggy had seen the hideous woman do it so many times before. Her mother, trying hard to please, had allowed Emily Gotobed to reserve 'a family burial plot' in the new pet cemetery for 'Darling,' herself and her husband, and Alicia Duncan Forbes had wind of it.

'It'll be over my dead body...you haven't heard the last of this!' shrieked The Bitch Queen, wagging her jewelled finger at the poor defenceless woman.

It was compulsive, and at the same time, repulsive viewing. Alison Tipple was so apologetic she was begging Alicia Duncan Forbes to forgive her and was stammering just as she had as a child. When the Pearly Gates front door had finally closed, Tiggy watched as her mother slumped into a corner and wept. The Rainbow Child fought back her own tears anxious to see what would happen next. The screen went blank before flashing again as Millie B appeared dressed, as usual, in boy's clothes. The little girl was hiding in a cupboard under the stairs, shaking and sobbing.

'Pl...pl...Please d...Don't,' the girl stammered repeatedly.

Her eyes were puffy and red as if she had been crying for hours. Tiggy wanted to reach out to her but the image swiftly changed again. The Wobniar's eyes were burning into her as she continued to stare at the screen, the importance of what was happening clearly etched upon his face. This time Millie A appeared trying to sleep on a stone floor. The young boy was huddled inside an old corn sack, with a rolled-up jumper for a pillow. Millie A was shivering, blue with cold. It was a bed unfit for a dog. The Wobniar waved his sabre with purposeful strokes and the screen went blank, the golden pot gleaming just as it had before.

'Your time as a Rainbow Child is coming to an end. The Crystal Keeper is ready to release the powers from 'The Crystals of Change,' The Wobniar announced pointing his sabre at the chameleon, and it obediently scuttled forward.

'This is your Crystal Keeper,' he said. 'The Crystals of Change have been loaned to you during your journey as a Rainbow Child. It is now time to sacrifice them to your Crystal Keeper so that their powers may be yours.'

Tiggy fumbled in her kangaroo pouch and feeling the crystals' rough edges, passed them one at a time to the chameleon. With each crystal received, the creature's scaly skin changed colour to match. Red, orange, yellow, green, blue, indigo and violet, she parted with them all until only The Stig Man's rock of midnight blue remained in her pouch. Suddenly, The Pot of Gold's screen flashed again. This time, the Derbyshire's mill and the lake of tears came into focus. Both of The Millies were present, staring into the water as if searching for a reflection that was not there.

Only Millie B's straw hat floated on the surface. Tiggy watched the children, her friends all summer, hunched over double by the weight of heavy sacks on their backs, and she felt sad to see that they were both still crying.

'Let the healing begin and seal the fate of this Rainbow Child,' boomed The Wobniar in a masterful voice.

Tiggy felt the jelly return to her knees, fearful of the unknown and what awaited her. However, it did not last for long as Angel Seraphina smiled through her body and held her steadfast, fixing Tiggy's eyes to The Pot of Gold's screen once more.

'Dry the tears and heal the past, bury the burden and set them free!' The Wobniar cried.

The Crystal Keeper responded, unleashing its massive rolled-up tongue and flicking each of the crystals upwards.

'Ops, Felicitas, Spes, Salus, Fortuna, Virtus, Pax' The Guardian of the Rainbow roared.

The Pot of Gold's screen briefly flashed followed by one almighty splash. The crystals had landed and disappeared inside the pot and mystically reappeared on the screen, landing into the lake.

'I don't believe it!' mumbled Tiggy under her breath as she watched the pool of tears rapidly begin to shrink on the screen.

The heavy sacks upon The Millies' backs were also collapsing and becoming lighter. The smaller the sacks, the more upright the children became until eventually the sacks were completely empty and they were standing up straight. They had stopped crying and their faces were changing too. It seemed unbelievable, beyond her wildest imagination: The Millies were ageing by the second, growing up before her eyes...fresh faced children morphing almost grotesquely into adults.

'It can't be!' Tiggy gasped. 'Mum!....Father! How can this be possible?' she asked moving closer, stunned by what she was seeing. 'It is them! It actually is!'

Tiggy reached out to the screen but her parents images had vaporised. The Wobniar nodded in approval.

'It is done!' he declared and stroking her feet with his crystal sabre.

Tiggy's footprints instantly melted, becoming sealed into the golden dust. Her time at The Rainbow's End was complete but her footprints would be there forever like those of the other Rainbow Children to have gone before.

'Please take care of Arthur for me,' said The Wobniar

staring at his prodigy. 'Ask him to let everyone know that the curse has been lifted. The Crystals of Change, YOUR Crystals of Change did that. You should feel very proud, Tiggy Tipple, of your time here. Also, please tell Arthur not to go out in the storm and that it is okay for him to cut his hair.'

A robin from the flock hopped onto his shoulder.

'I need to visit him more,' said The Wobniar stroking the bird with his sabre as if he was blessing it. 'I shall be sending my robin more often to see him. Please tell him!'

Tiggy's surprised green eyes stared back at this wizardly man looking for the first time beyond his crazy hair and ghostly skin. Her friend, Arthur Ramsbottom flashed into her mind, Mrs. Derbyshire's newspaper cuttings, the lightning tree, the terrible storm, and the missing boy. Everything made sense.

Arthur Ramsbottom's long lost twin moved his sabre again tapping her on her shoulder blades and Tiggy instantly felt her body lighten. Angel Seraphina blessed her with a cascade of white feathers, one of which floated down to land upon her head. A silky sensation stroked Tiggy across the width of her back and although it only lasted a few seconds for that brief moment, she felt the presence of wings.

Chapter 27

AFTER THE RAINBOW

Life changed after The Rainbow's End for Tiggy and her family, and her trips to the woods were never quite the same as they had been that long, hot summer. Tiggy had lost her bike to the shadows of her parents' past but in its place, she had found new hope for a brighter future. In any case, she had perfected the Superman before her bike had hit the skip.

When Tiggy returned to the Derbyshire's mill, the surrounding farmland was bone dry. After weeks of the land being strangely flooded, there was now not a sign that the water had ever been there. The images on The Pot of Gold had been true: both the water and The Millies were gone and only a straw hat remained. Tiggy knew it belonged to Millie B but thought she had also seen the hat somewhere else before and racked her brains trying to think just where. For two days, it had sent her nearly insane, but then Tiggy remembered the old photograph that she had found in the attic of 'George, aged 7,' holding a panda and wearing the same sort of hat. She realised that as unlikely as it was, the boater belonged to the 'George' in the photograph. Tiggy mulled it over in her head thinking about how at The Rainbow's End she had seen Millie B, dressed as a boy morph into her mother. She remembered how on the night that Pants had gone missing her mother had confided that the panda had previously been her very own Mr. Sixty, and that as a child she had been treated like a boy and called George. For Tiggy it was a 'joining the dots' revelation that the boater belonged to her mother and it was she who was the child in the photograph holding the panda. Tiggy wanted that hat. However, when she went to touch it, like her parents' image on The Pot of Gold, the hat too vaporised in front of her. It was as if it had never existed. Nevertheless, the jigsaw puzzle, like her journey, was now finally complete.

For several days, Tiggy returned to the mill hoping to find The Millies again, but it was misplaced optimism and she knew it. It had been quite a long and drawn-out affair getting the film developed from her instamatic, but when after a couple of weeks the wallet of photographs finally arrived back in the post, Tiggy was excited to have something that would keep the memories of her friends alive. She had taken many photographs of them but to her surprise and disappointment, neither the mill children nor the puddle appeared on a single one. In fact, they were not on the negatives either. The mill children were not real, never had been and only Tiggy as a chosen Rainbow Child had been able to see them. The Millies were simply a restless energy from her parents' troubled childhoods. The Tipple children had often wondered about their parents' past, but like the best-kept secrets, it had been a past shrouded in mystery. Now she understood why. It had been a past too painful to face.

'Poor Mum and Dad! That puddle of tears was enormous! They must have been crying in their hearts for years!' Tiggy said to Pirate Pants who was back safely by her side.

Mrs. Derbyshire had found the beloved bear outside her yard on the morning that Tiggy had gone to The Indigo.

'You do realise, Pants that our friends, The Millies were never real like us. Only you and I could see them,' she said kissing the bear. They were just spirits made from Mum and Dads' unhappy childhoods. Do you understand?'

She pretended that the bear did not and made it shake its head.

'They had a lot of bad stuff happen to them and it made them sad. It's okay now though 'cos The Wobniar and me fixed it,' she said cuddling the bear tightly so that he could not possibly escape. 'It's all thanks to Angel Seraphina. She's the one who picked me to be a Rainbow Child.'

Tiggy was right. She knew what she had seen. The spirit children themselves had been the result of an unhappy and brooding energy. She was sad knowing that she would never see her dear friends, The Millies, again, but she could only feel a deep happiness that the demons from her parents' troubled childhoods had gone. Theirs had been a heavy burden, like the sacks upon the spirit children's backs. The sacks were emotional baggage they did not need and it had stopped them from moving on and living. It had weighed them down and made them unable to be themselves or to find the joy in life. At the Rainbow's End Tiggy had watched the spirit children's sacks disappear and now she understood them so much more.

'Those sacks are empty now though, Pirate Pants. Now they can be happy. The Crystals of Change set them free. Have you noticed how different they are? Mum even lets you sit at the meal table!' Tiggy said adjusting Pant's eye patch. She looked at the bear and considered the patch.

'You don't need this anymore! It's who you are!' she said to Pants removing the patch. 'Mr. Sheepsbottom says it's our imperfections that make us perfect,' and she kissed the spot where Pant's eye was missing. With or without an eye it didn't change how she thought about him.

It was a new beginning. Just as the sun had gone down to stay on her parents' past, the events of The Rainbow's End had brought a new dawn for the Tipple family. They understood each other, not minding that they thought differently about stuff. It no longer mattered that Tiggy was a girl who sometimes behaved a lot like a boy. There was no longer a pressure to 'grow out of it,' as The Greygoyles suggested. They were each free and happy to be their true selves and even to dream and to chase them.

At first, the changes at Number 6 were only small. Downstairs, out went Spring Bouquet and in came mugs and ketchup. Upstairs, Thomas and Alison Tipple shared both a bedroom and a bed and the children had posters on their bedroom walls. Alex had chosen one of the 'The Milky Way' (the space kind and not the chocolate bar!) and another of David Bowie as 'Ziggy Stardust,' Penelope's posters were of ballerinas and pointe shoes and Tiggy had opted for BMX champions and their bikes, and another of a mole wearing a workman's yellow hard hat. She had made sure her father had seen how endearing it looked and it had seemed to work because he no longer worried about molehills springing up. In the garden, a weed could also now survive at least a day or two and the buddleia living up to its 'butterfly bush' nickname, was brimming with butterflies. The bush had never had so many before as Alex was swift to point out.

'All these Lepidoptewa can only mean one thing. There's going to be a lot of change awound here,' he said staring at a black and orange butterfly that had landed on the book he was holding.

Things were different away from the home, too. The library visits still happened but they also did stuff where popcorn and ice cream were involved and ate chip shop chips in the car even where The Greygoyles could see them. Everything was far more chilled and all the happier for it. Thomas Tipple in particular, was now working to live instead of living to work and fewer jobs were being 'jobbed.' He also, having hidden a secret desire, ever since he was a boy, had now 'come out of the shed' so to speak. He no longer skulked off in the dead of night to dress up in leathers and look at motorbike magazines, but did so in full view of his family. At heart, Thomas Tipple was a boy racer, a born-again biker, except that he had never owned one in the first place. However, he did now. 'Father', who was now called 'Dad' by his girls, (although to Alex he was 'Major Tom' named after the astronaut in David Bowie's song.) was the very proud owner of a high handle-barred beast of a machine, and more importantly, his wife did not object.

These days Alison Tipple was like a different woman. She had started using her first name, Georgina, again although at home she insisted on her husband calling her Georgie. The liberated woman had shrugged off her shadowy past; out went the suit of shame worn beneath the frumpy clothes and in came a trendier image with a softer, more 'with it' hairstyle and without the lacquer. There had always been an attractive woman hidden beneath it all. Her new confident self rocked all the latest fashions and even a pair of tight, bottom-hugging jeans on her 'scruff' days. Georgina Tipple had discovered denim and it suited her. She certainly wasn't bothered about having expensive shoes any more.

'Who cares what the neighbours think!' she said wearing one of her husband's shirts to paint their new bedroom.

She had paint all over it and in her hair despite it being in a slightly untidy bun.

'Messy hair, don't care!' she said under her breath before answering the door to a Greygoyle.

In fact, they were becoming her favourite things to say. Nothing that Tiggy did or said upset her either. The porcelain figurine was powerless. Georgina Tipple now moved it off the spot herself.

'What on earth are you doing Mumsibums!' Tiggy quipped trying out a cheeky new name having noticed what her mother had done.

'Off centre is good. I prefer it like that!' replied Georgina as she walked away chuckling, 'Mumsibums!' she repeated under her breath, 'Love it! I actually do!'

The neat freak had left the building and thanks to the sodalite crystal from The Indigo Realm, so too had her nervous stammer that had been well and truly cured.

However, the big changes came on the eve of Tiggy's tenth birthday. Tiggy was in her bedroom with Pants moulding a bubble gum monster of James Cartwright. At the man's request, the undertaker had measured him for his coffin every month for over a year but James Cartwright was still 'in God's waiting room' as he constantly reminded anyone who would listen. Tiggy opened her bedroom window and looked out onto the garden. The buddleia bush by the potting shed was once again a mass of butterflies. Alex had taught her all about them in a recent 'catch up lesson.' The orange brought joy, the white were from angels, the blue were 'the wish granters' and the purple were so rare and special that she simply would never see one. A sighting of a purple butterfly for anyone lost on their path in life meant that a transformation was about to occur. The Stig Man's midnight blue rock twinkled on her windowsill. Apart from Pants, the chunk of lapis lazuli was her most prized possession. It took her back to the Indigo and to 'that last time'. Every night before bed, she held the stone and said words of thanks and appreciation similar to a bedtime prayer.

'I wish for The Stig Man to be safe and back home again. Thank you for your help, for saving me, for being my friend and for giving me this stone as a reminder of our friendship.'

The stone made her feel both happy and sad at the same time. As Rainbow Children, they had shared an extraordinary journey of body and mind, the memories constantly sweeping in and out of her consciousness. They were like the tides of the sea, sometimes turbulent and fearsome, at other times calm and peaceful. However, they were always there, an enduring force beyond control. There was no doubt that the boy had reserved a special place in her heart. Somehow, somewhere, Tiggy desperately hoped to meet The Stig Man again.

She gazed out onto her sunflowers in Arthur Ramsbottom's garden. Next year things would be different. Her father had promised to give the children room to grow their own and there would be a prize for the tallest. Tiggy's photographs that she had taken that summer were scattered on her bed. Arthur Ramsbottom was on several of them and so too were her sunflowers, but the rosy glow that she had so often seen surrounding his body was not there. However, something else was, although it was so faint and ghostly that she wondered if she was imagining it. A young boy about her age, wearing an old coat and hobnail boots was standing right next to Arthur Ramsbottom on every single photograph. Could it really be his long-lost twin brother, Arnold? She thought that it probably was.

She wished The Stig Man could be with her to celebrate her birthday and reaching double digits. Her 10th birthday felt such a big one. Tiggy looked at The Stig Man's rock on her windowsill and could hardly believe her eyes. A magnificent purple butterfly had flown in through the open window and nestled upon the stone.

What an incredible summer it had been and still it was not quite over. Tiggy could hear bits and bobs of a conversation coming from downstairs. Alicia Duncan Forbes was on the doorstep. She was the smug bearer of bad news. Earlier that evening, 'Darling', the Gotobeds' thought to be human poodle, had been in the couples' newly installed sunken whirlpool bath, when Emily Gotobed had attempted to remove her choker from the dog's neck in order to dry its hair. The poodle had viciously snapped, biting her on the arm and the working hairdryer had fallen out of Emily Gotobed's hand into the scented bathwater.

'Darling has been electrocuted! Goodness gracious!' Georgina Tipple exclaimed horrified that the dog had met such a grisly ending.

Alicia Duncan Forbes could not have cared less.

'Didn't I tell you that it was always going to end in tears!' she said smirking and suddenly noticing a ring on Georgina Tipple's hand that she had never seen before.

It was a surprise gift from Thomas to his wife, an exquisite clear watery-blue stone, surrounded by a dozen sparkling diamonds. Apart from her simple gold curtain ring style wedding band it was the only ring that Georgina had ever owned. For the first time in his life, Thomas had been truly extravagant and had acted on impulse. He saw it, he liked it and he bought it! Alicia Duncan Forbes looked shocked.

'Is it real?' she enquired smiling falsely through gritted teeth.

'Oh yes, down to the very last diamond,' said Georgina proudly holding out her hand for Alicia Duncan Forbes to take a closer look.

The Heavenly Gardens 'Queen of Bling' could hardly bring herself to do so.

'Isn't it nice that you have a ring that you can wear every day,' said a peeved Alicia. 'Of course, the trouble with mine is that most of them are worth so much money that I just never dare wear them...the insurance alone would cost much more than your ring ...'

Suddenly, and most unexpectedly Georgina flipped.

'What a wicked, evil old bag you are! Just take yourself and your vulgar jewellery back to your sad little life and leave us alone!' said Georgina calmly. 'Oh! By the way, Alicia...those heels,' she said, staring down at the woman's colossal feet, 'are just so last season!' and coolly shut the door in her face.

Alicia Duncan Forbes was so shocked that her clumsy feet got the better of her and losing her balance fell backwards into a wheelbarrow of horse manure, which Thomas had been digging into the garden.

It was of course an act of social suicide for the Tipples. Their good standing from being long-time, polite dogsbodies for The Greygoyles was shattered in seconds. Alicia Duncan Forbes was a heavy weight of influence amongst The Greygoyles. She was most definitely not a good person to fall out with, even though nobody really liked her. However, Georgina Tipple, unlike Alison Tipple, no longer seemed to care.

The following day was Tiggy's 10th birthday and her mother had organised their very first party at Pearly Gates. She had gone a bit mad with the invitations and virtually every child in the village had one. She even allowed the undesirables, Mikey Mucus and Toadie to gate-crash.

'They're wight cwetins. Whatever are you thinking! They will wuin it!' Alex complained.

He adjusted his Ziggy Stardust costume and looked out of the window. Both boys were on Mikey's chopper bike and roaring with laughter as Toadie dropped his trousers to show his bare buttocks off to the close. The new tape deck was blasting out all of Alex's favourite Bowie songs and despite several complaints from The Greygoyles Georgina Tipple had refused to turn it down.

Mrs. Derbyshire arrived at teatime with a huge homemade birthday cake that had ten candles and a cute little black Labrador puppy for the family to keep.

'What about Armstwong or Buzz?' Alex said trying to think of a name. 'it 'ud be ace to name him after the first men to walk on the moon. Or perhaps, Apollo after their wocket? Not the Gweek god!'

Just then, the tape recorder changed track and started to play David Bowie's 'Starman.' The little puppy barked for the first time.

'I think he likes it!' said Penelope.

'Starman Bowie!' What a terwific name!' Alex said stroking the puppy's velvety ears.

'Bowie for short!' added Penelope kissing the top of its head. The puppy barked again, wagging his tail as if it approved. The little Labrador had its name.

However, Starman Bowie aside, Mrs. Derbyshire had also come with an interesting proposition. She had decided to go and live with her older sister in the next village and was looking for somebody to take over the farmhouse.

'It would be rent free, no strings attached. There would be nothing to pay. The children could play out every day without you worrying,' she said picking up Bowie to give him a cuddle. 'This little chap would certainly love it!'

Mikey ran into the kitchen, pretending to bowl overarm and blowing a party blowout. He blew it again. The paper tube unrolled and made it's horn like noise right in front of Bowie's face but the little dog did not so much as flinch. Mikey ran away, fake bowling and disappointed.

'You certainly sent that little monkey away with his tail between his legs!' said Mrs. Derbyshire, stroking Bowie. The two women laughed. 'So, what do you think about the idea? There is nobody I would rather live there than you lovely people. Have a think about it!'

Balloons, party blowouts, cheese and pineapple on sticks, jelly and blancmange and an excitable cute little black Labrador puppy were all things that a few weeks earlier Tiggy could not have imagined in her wildest dreams. Tiggy had never felt so happy.

'This can't get any better!' she whispered to Bowie, already completely in love with him.

However, she had absolutely no idea what was in store for her until it was her turn to pin the tail on the donkey. She was nowhere close with her tail but when the blindfold had been removed, her father had wheeled a gleaming brand-new stunts bicycle into the room decorated with the biggest bow imaginable. Tiggy opened the envelope tied to its seat and inside was a note from her father handwritten in indigo coloured ink. It read:

'Don't follow where the path may lead. Go instead where there is no path and leave a trail.'

'Defo!' Tiggy said, and they both smiled.

One week later Harry 'Flash' Dobson was on his doorstep polishing his brass knocker in his usual lightning fashion. The Gotobeds were with him showing off 'Princess,' their new poodle. The little dog yapped. Emily Gotobed gestured to her husband to pass her handbag. She swiftly removed a baby's pacifier and stuffed the dummy into the young poodle's mouth, adjusted it's pink tutu, before going on their way to complete another circuit of the close.

Arthur Ramsbottom was just back from the barbers with a short new hair cut when he spotted Tiggy on her new bike. A robin was by his feet and was so tame it hopped onto Arthur Ramsbottom's shoe.

'My two favourite visitors!' said Arthur smiling at Tiggy and pointing to the robin. 'This one has started coming to see me every day,' he said bending down to the little bird. 'I think he's a fan of your sunflowers.'

'I think we both really know why he visits. He's checking up on you,' said Tiggy smiling at the robin and thinking how much he must have missed his twin brother over the years.

'I'm so glad Arnold told you that the curse has been lifted,' said Arthur 'it's just a shame that nobody believes it, but time will prove it. It always does.'

Arthur Ramsbottom and Tiggy walked over to the flowers and the robin followed and began to sing. The sunflowers had been spectacular all summer long but were now in their last flushes of colour. Things were different. The old man's pink outer haze had gone whilst the sickly sunflower, having belatedly found its strength, was now much taller than Tiggy and was in full flowering glory.

'Didn't I tell you that all it needed was TLC and a little patience?' said Arthur Ramsbottom.

Tiggy nodded, smiling and as she did so, a snowy white feather came seemingly from nowhere and landed at her feet.

'Angel Seraphina!' she said under her breath.

Next door, Penelope and Alex were about to take Bowie for a walk. Alex was wearing his new moon boots because he couldn't wait for winter to try them. He was singing David Bowie's "Space Oddity" to Bowie thinking that the puppy would like it as much as he did.

'Let's go!' Tiggy said joining them from the Ramsbottoms on her new stunts cycle.

Penelope climbed on the back and off they went. A white butterfly fluttered up the road after them and landed on Tiggy's shoulder.

'Wait for us!' shouted Alex running to catch them up with Bowie on his lead.

The children passed by the Luvvies. They had just uprooted their newly planted fir trees that were now lying on the path. Their living room window was wide open and the children could see inside. The parrot was in its cage watching them from its perch.

'Gwound contwol to Major Tom,' Alex sang loudly to see if the parrot would react.

'Noisy brat! Noisy brat!' the Luvvie's parrot squawked.

The children laughed and were still laughing when they passed the local estate agent heading for Pearly Gates with a For Sale sign to display. The weather had changed and a heavy black cloud hung over the close, the first spits and spots of rain were beginning to fall. A storm was on its way. As the last traces of sunshine streaked through the inky cloud, its silver silhouette cast a magical light over Pearly Gates.

'There will do nicely,' said Thomas to the estate agent pointing to a spot in the front garden by a huge molehill. 'That's another jo...' and he stopped himself.

The estate agent was still banging in the 'For Sale' sign when moments later, Thomas Tipple roared out of the close on his motorbike and chuckled to himself as he saw the wave of net curtains twitch.

ABOUT THE AUTHOR

Amanda Ryan grew up in rural Norfolk, England enjoying the outdoors, making secret dens and hurtling along on the back of her brother's racing bike. It was a work driven, sporty household and anything her brothers did, Amanda did too whether it was playing cricket, boxing or fruit picking for pocket money. Her dolls' pram transported anything but a doll, and her 'go everywhere bear' was precisely just that. In summer, she raced her shadow across the lawn at a time when she also believed that their garden peas grew in cans in their vegetable patch. She loved that world of make-believe that has never abandoned her.

Married with four children, Amanda met her husband Greg at school. She believes that childhood is a time for exploration, and on encountering the autistic spectrum for the first time, she soon realised the value in focussing on strengths (and there are many and wonderful) rather than weaknesses and that there are hidden gems of inspiring talent waiting to be discovered and nurtured to their true potential. Amanda has several years' experience of both voluntary home-schooling (she called it 'Pink School') as well as navigating the traditional school system for children with special educational needs with successful outcomes. She always hoped to inject as much magic as possible into their early years with Easter bunny garden deliveries at dawn (the alarm clock had to be set for that one!) and madcap birthday parties that the guests, now grown up, still talk and laugh about to this day. More than anything, she encouraged her children to pursue their dreams and to say 'I can' rather than 'I can't.'

Amanda loves rainbows, painting pebbles, eating chip shop chips in the car, woodland walks with Bowie and the untamed sea in inclement weather. Since Covid 19 Lockdown, she has planted thousands of autumn bulbs as the sleeping guardians of hope for new life in the spring. She loves skiing and the zingy mountain air and is always the first outside to build a snowman (or even a snow panda!) and the child in her is still very much alive.

Amanda loves hearing from her readers.
You can write to her at amandagreg6@aol.com